PILLOW TALK

The Legend of Lorelie Begins

by Daria Wagoner

ACKNOWLEDGEMENTS

Tanya Wagoner - My precious Sister and Guardian Angel. "I miss you so much."
Tori Harter - One of my best friends who watches now from above,
with a tender spirit.
Suzanne Rares - I am sure that you are settling your score with "Siri," in Heaven,
my brownie-loving Friend, except remember that she was right on one thing,
"Chocolate is the meaning of life! "

***

Jedediah and Patricia Wagner - My courageous son, and his beautiful wife.
Cynthia Macgregor - Editor and friend.
Michelle Soule' " Graphics Extraordinaire! " For the great cover art,
guidance, and friendship.
Hector Noel - A true and crazy friend. One of the most intelligent men I have ever met.
The Staff at Photographics USA, in Stuart, Florida

***

To "JL"- I owe much to this special person whose love and caring ways have truly
been an inspiration.
The never-ending opportunities for humor have kept me laughing through
burned hot dogs and, ill-fitting sarongs

***

I wish to also acknowledge the brave individuals who continue to give so much to help
the abandoned, abused, and neglected animals, which remain in need
as a result of recent hurricanes.
Theirs is a soulful burden I share, and I promise to do whatever I possibly can
to make things better, and to leave this World a better place for all.
Thanks, Jessica Nicodemo, Nick Barson, and all of the other beautiful people
involved in "Rescue Life."

***

And a final acknowledgment of gratitude to the Guardian of Giants, in Puerto Rico.
Luis Gonzales Horse and Pony Rescue
"Where love, hope, and dedication make miracles a reality."

Contents

Sexual Survey Results
Please take the time to read the answers to
an anonymous sexual survey that was designed to make
readers think about various sexual situations across the
lifespan, for both men and women.
This was a non-scientific study... and meant
only to enlighten and entertain. So... ENJOY!!!

Chapter 1
A Wild Weekend to Remember

With the sun nearly setting on an early Friday evening in fall, Deidre relaxed on her porch, sipping a cocktail, while contemplating the night she wanted to have. She was grateful that she was off duty for the long upcoming weekend. It's been way too long, she thought to herself, feeling that warm, throbbing sensation between her legs as a reminder.

The work week had been a tough one, with Thanksgiving and Christmas not too far off. But Deidre did not want to think now about the holidays, or the additional work they inevitably involved. On this long weekend off, she wanted and needed a break. Deidre knew the stressors were only going to be compounded once the holidays arrived, bringing added depression to exacerbate the already-complex psyche issues that surround that time of year, and she was not looking forward to it.

Deidre's psychology practice was thriving, which was wonderful financially, but she knew she needed some serious stress relief in order to remain on top of her game. It was becoming difficult to listen to some of the stories and other rants of her patients day after day, and she felt herself growing irritable at times when she knew she should not. Deidre often felt this way when she was not getting enough intimate, carnal relief, almost as if she had some sort of barometer in her psyche, causing her to become easily intolerant when her overwhelming physical needs were not being met. At times Deidre thought that she, herself, needed therapy, but the only therapy she really required this evening could be provided by a man.

"Shall I make a phone call?" she asked herself aloud, teasingly. To be sure, it was a rhetorical question. Deidre had not needed to call any of her boy toys in some time, but her sexual appetite was growing ravenous once again, and she had grown weary of resorting to satisfying herself with her favorite toys. She had jokingly told her stockbroker and long-time friend, Sally, that she was considering buying stock in Duracell and Energizer, since she used so many batteries. Though the remark had made them both laugh, the underlying truth was serious. Deidre knew she needed a real man to satiate her unrelenting sexual desire this night.

Frustrated by the lack of one partner who was her equal both sexually and intellectually, she resorted to frequent soirées with various men of even more varying ages. It was a haphazard and potentially dangerous way to fill the void, she knew, until her Prince Charming would come along. But in her heart, Deidre seriously doubted that there would ever be one viable suitor, for she knew that she could be difficult to deal with at times and even harder to live with. Deidre felt she could somehow relate to Constance's plight, as portrayed in D.H. Lawrence's novel Lady Chatterley's Lover, in that intelligence alone was not enough.

Years of listening to her patients and their stories had left Deidre somewhat jaded, intolerant of nonsense, while she worried even in her after-hours about a patient named Katrina, a young new mother struggling with issues of adapting to motherhood while suffering with schizophrenia. Katrina had not shown up for her scheduled appointment today, nor could Deidre reach her, causing her great concern for both Katrina and her infant. If she did not hear from her soon, she would make a call to a friend of hers within the police department to stop in for a welfare check on Katrina. She so needed a distraction from it all, even for just a little while, to refuel for the tough months that lay ahead.

Now fifty years of age, Deidre had always held her own in every facet of her life, appearing to be on top of the world to those she worked and socialized with, and in most ways she was—except for one. Deidre's many accomplishments were both a badge of honor as well as a double-edged sword, leaving many a man out in the cold, unable to keep up with her complex and quirky personality. The younger men were attracted to her youthful and exciting lifestyle and appearance, while the older men seemed drawn to her freely independent and uninhibited nature, lacking in pretense.

Deidre knew that in spite of lacking a real boyfriend, she definitely lived a life that most women could only dream about and would never dare to speak of, at least where the sex was concerned. She had already listened to so many frustrated men and women speak of their mundane lives and relationships with very little sex, many times performed only out of a sense of duty. She knew that theirs was a life she did not understand, nor could she live with. Sex was a frequently needed aspect of life for Deidre, and she felt that if her disgruntled patients would speak more about it with their own partners, they would not need her services so often.

There were a few freaky patients Deidre had who crossed the line when it came to sex, however, bordering on perversion even by her standards. Danny Cameron was one of those oddities. Deidre had to choose her wardrobe even more carefully when Danny was on the schedule. Danny had been court-ordered into therapy for his sexual predilections after a recent incident landing him in legal trouble with multiple counts of sexually related charges.

Realizing that Danny would experience uncontrollable erotomanic delusions frequently during his manic-depressive episodes, Deidre had to dress as matronly as was possible, in addition to being extra cautious when responding and reacting to his grandiose tales of women who he was sure wanted him, and then exposing his genitals to the unsuspecting women.

Early on, Deidre had had to set hard and fast boundaries with Danny, due to his constant sexual innuendos and lack of respect for others' personal space. She was exhausted after her sessions with Danny, and the bedroom stories he seemingly enjoyed recanting during therapy, watching her intently for a reaction. Deidre felt her own sexual activities, as exciting as they were, paled in comparison to Danny's, thankfully, but Deidre's secret sex life was exciting all the same.

Deidre had had her most recent ménage à trois, with two men, just several weeks earlier and often reflected on what an absolute blast it had been to spend three nights and four days with the two of them. During the days, the trio played carelessly naked aboard a large boat in the ocean, while each night brought intense sexual sessions she enjoyed so much and now missed. I would love to do that at least once more! Deidre thought.

Stopping off for a drink at a local dive bar with her girlfriend Sandra one evening, two handsome and well-dressed men arrived and sat themselves on the opposite side of the bar, from the vixens. They glanced curiously over at Deidre and her friend, who were dressed provocatively and ready for an action-packed night on the town.

As part of their plan to meet the two handsome creatures on the other side of the bar, Sandra carried her cell phone over to the seated men with an alluring smile and asked them to take a picture of Deidre and herself. The two sirens believed their simple plan to be an effective means in breaking the ice for conversation. But once the provocatively posed pictures were taken of Deidre and Sandra, Sandra curiously scooted over to speak with a clearly transgender man seated several stools down at the bar, leaving Deidre all alone in the company of the two men. She didn't mind a bit.

Making affirmative eye contact with the two men from across the bar, Deidre left her seat and approached the pair. The sexual energy and desire that Deidre felt flowing between her legs in the presence of these two was dizzying. There was going to be some sort of action tonight, she knew—she just didn't know with which one. They were both good looking, with chiseled faces to match their sculpted bodies, however, so it didn't matter too much to her which one she wound up with. Or just maybe I could have them both! she contemplated, with a sly grin began taking possession of her face. Sandra continued talking with her strange man, while Deidre took full advantage of the situation to get to know her two new prospective lovers, desiring all the attention for herself anyway.

As she neared the two men, Deidre smiled in approval, noting them both to be casually dressed in blue jeans with freshly ironed button-down shirts, open just enough at the top to tease her vivid imagination. "Well, hello there. My name is Deidre," she began, while observing and further analyzing the two. Mark introduced himself and his friend Rich, asking if he could buy her a drink and calling over the bartender.

With introductions out of the way, the three began probing each other further, with Deidre inquiring as to what sort of occupations they had. Mark said that his job required him to travel frequently, while his friend Rich, an architect, was down visiting from out-of-state. This was the first night of their annual "guys' weekend," Rich explained, laughing heartily in a telling manner. It was obvious that they were definitely planning a weekend of wicked debauchery, which Deidre wanted to know more about— and participate in.

Elaborating further, Mark commented that his friend Rich did not get to have much sex. "Oh what a shame!" Deidre responded in a sarcastically seductive manner, realizing her nipples had become erect with excitement at the thought of cavorting with the two, but she didn't want to make the first move or seem too easy. I could easily take care of that deficit, she thought.

The men scooted over, making room for Deidre to sit between them as they continued chatting. At first they made small talk, and then they talked about their jobs, finally bandying about suggestions for what to do for the rest of the evening. Deidre felt relieved that she and Sandra had each driven their own vehicles that night, leaving each free to do whatever they wished and with whomever they wanted.

Mark was the more outspoken of the two men, while Rich acted like more of a gentleman, Deidre thought, as they began asking Deidre details about her work and personal life. They seemed fascinated with the fact that she was a psychologist and questioned her about the types of patients she would see on a normal day, and other curious details. Although Deidre could not go into specific details, she could still give them a good idea without breaking any patient confidentiality.

Mark, Rich, and Deidre each had several cocktails as the conversation about Deidre's patients turned into sexual problems and proclivities. This is going to be a most interesting evening, Deidre thought as both Mark and Rich moved themselves in closer to her while they chatted. It was not long before she felt a hand on her right thigh, sending erotic shivers to all the right places.

The message Deidre was receiving from the two men was clear to her at that moment, and she could not be any more pleased. It was obvious that she would be spending this evening with Mark and Rich. Fantasies raced through her mind as Mark asked for their check and paid the bar tab.

"Why don't we go back to my place and get into the hot tub?" Mark suggested, a touch of uncertainty edging his voice as he watched and waited for Deidre's response to his invitation. Little did Mark and Rich know, that Deidre was already pondering playful activities, which the night might have in store for them. Wild thoughts caused every hair on her body to stand on end, and now feeling an increasing wetness in her most private areas. Deidre shifted on the barstool in eager anticipation of the night's festivities.

Writing down his phone number and address, Mark handed the information to Deidre, suggesting that she follow them this first time so as not to get lost. Being somewhat familiar with the nice area his home was in, Deidre knew it to be not far off. She felt completely at ease with both men, sensing them to be just horny and sex deprived. Deidre had become quite adept at "reading" her men after many years of practice, both professionally and personally.

Deidre walked over to Sandra, who was heartily laughing at something the offbeat man had said, to let her know where she was going, then left the bar to follow Mark's Mercedes for the ten-minute car ride.

Mark's home reflected the life of a normal single father, clean and well organized, with pictures of his children adorning the walls. He also had a beautiful boat docked in the water behind his home. It could be seen through the sliding glass doors, which led out to a large screened-in porch with a pool, party-sized hot tub, wet bar, and lounging area, which she immediately realized were well thought out. Mark appeared so far to be someone who took pride in his home and family, Deidre admiringly concluded.

After the usual formalities of showing Deidre around the home, the three assembled in the kitchen to make cocktails, while Mark spoke of taking the boat out for a cruise in the ocean the next morning and asking Deidre to join them. "Absolutely! I love the ocean!" Deidre replied with excitement.

"Awesome! Then plan on joining us. It will be fun—and the weather is supposed to be gorgeous, too!" Mark added.

The three stood in the kitchen in an awkward yet sexually charged moment of analytical silence. "I'll be right back," Mark said, leaving Deidre and Rich in the kitchen to cue up some music on the stereo in the living room. Mark seemed unconcerned about leaving the two alone.

Rich did not waste any time in approaching Deidre, engaging her in a passion-filled kiss, feeling her body with his hands through her clothes, while pressing himself into her so that she

11

could feel his very hard and erect penis. My, you really are ready! Deidre thought, as Rich's exploration escalated in intensity. She felt him wanting to consume her right there and then, as the two stood in an entanglement in the kitchen. Though the oven is off, it's sure hot in here! Deidre's mind mentioned.

Within a few moments, Mark returned to the kitchen, joining Rich and Deidre just as the song "I Want Your Sex," could be heard resonating throughout the house on the surround-sound system. Deidre was so ready to get the evening started, hearing George Michaels's sultry voice singing the seductive lyrics about wanting sex.

This was exactly what Deidre had desired and dreamed of, she thought, as both men affectionately caressed and simultaneously fondled her from both front and back, leaving no sensitivity-heightened area unexplored. Deidre, now in a euphoric state of ecstasy, became acutely aware of strong hands coming around from behind her, starting at her thighs and slowly working their way upward, tantalizing her, as they meandered their way up and around her chest to finally land on her breasts, which responded immediately to the sensation. Deidre released a heavy sigh, wanting more.

Rich's rock-hard penis now pressed even more firmly inward, against Deidre's inviting backside, relaying a clear message of what his intentions were for her, while Mark claimed his place in front of Deidre, staring wantonly at her. With her eyes closed against further distraction, Deidre gyrated her pelvis backward in rhythm to both Rich's obvious bulge and the sensual sounds of sighs and music, mixed with the hormonal sweat.

With each arousing and seductive twist of her hips, Deidre could feel yet another hand venturing into places that had needed exactly this kind of attention for so long, her body and mind in complete agreement with the activity and pleasure she felt, and even more with the night that, she could only imagine at the moment, lay ahead. Erotic thoughts and ideas raced through her mind as the sexual song continued to play in the background, perfectly chosen for the moment, Deidre thought.

Feeling an animalistic drive for greater passion, Deidre opened her eyes to see Mark's carnal desire for her reflected in his eyes, adding further to the heightened excitement, nearing crescendo level. Ever so slowly, Deidre's hand wandered down Mark's chest and lower abdomen, noting each rippled muscle, which she could feel quiver in response to her teasing touch. Stopping just at the waistband of his jeans each time, her hand felt the need to explore farther. Let's start getting down to the good stuff, Deidre mused to herself, finally sliding her hand down his jeans until she just reached the tip of his penis, and then stopping. I can't let him get off this easily, she told herself, deciding to tease him a bit longer. Deidre gloried in knowing that she was the one in charge of the night.

Unable to resist temptation any longer, Deidre began massaging his throbbing rod through his pants, until she could take no more. Mark stood frozen, observing Deidre with pleasure, as she unbuckled his belt and unzipped his pants, allowing them to drop to the floor. Rich busied himself slipping Deidre's shirt off and unclasping her bra, unleashing her breasts to further tantalizing torment as well as the cooler night air, which brought her nipples to full attention as if begging for more.

Deidre could see Mark's penis's rigidity, with a bead of moisture already in place on its tip, which would ensure easy entry. She caressed his penis further, as Rich reached around Deidre from behind, unbuttoning her jean skirt, allowing it to fall to the floor to join the other intermingled garments that already lay there. She now stood nearly nude between the two men, with only her lacy thong panties, which barely cloaked her fit frame, shrouding her most private of play areas. Mark leaned down and gently slid Deidre's panties down with precision and ease.

13

With all of their clothing now in a heap in the middle of the kitchen floor, the trio became entwined, with both men kissing and sucking Deidre delicately, while wandering hands continued on their path, which knew no boundaries, in exploration of each other's body, but with Deidre's being the center of focus, much to her delicious delight.

This is a scenario that is only a fleeting fantasy for most, Deidre thought, and I can't think of anywhere else I'd rather be right now. She gloated at the privilege of being part of this highly sensual scene. Every ounce of her being was now crying out in starvation for satiation, which she knew she would soon have.

"Let's take this to the bedroom," Mark said softly, entering her wetness with a single finger as Rich continued sucking on one of her breasts while gently twisting and pulling the other nipple with his fingers, sending a most erotic shivering sensation coursing up Deidre's spine.

Yes! Finally! Deidre thought to herself, as the three walked naked through the living room and down the hallway to Mark's bedroom, with a king-size bed, which Deidre knew would be well used that night.

Three wanton bodies willed themselves into pleasurable positions spontaneously and carelessly, without inhibition or shame. This was an aspect of growing older that Deidre greatly appreciated, heightening her own urge and sexuality, she knew. She wasted no time in mounting Mark's increasingly rigid rod, slowly lowering herself down onto him to its hilt. Mark, now deep inside, held onto Deidre's hips as she rocked her pelvis back and forth, enjoying and appreciating each and every inch of length and girth of his joystick. She then began raising and lowering herself down onto him, slowly at first and then faster and faster, hearing his approving sighs and groans.

Rich had begun to stroke his tool while watching Deidre and Mark in action, anxiously awaiting his turn to be inside Deidre.

Not wanting Rich to be left out of the fun, Deidre summoned him to bring his fullness to her mouth, sucking him while continuing to move her pelvis up and down on Mark's cock until, in one final moment of sheer ecstasy, Mark would powerfully release himself into her.

That would be all Deidre needed to reach her own satiation. Now in sheer bliss, Deidre threw her head back and braced herself for her wonderfully emerging orgasm. "Yes! Yes! Yes!" she cried out loud, her entire body trembling with delirious delight.

Rich, nearby with his hard cock in hand, was ready and anxiously awaiting his own release now. He guided Deidre to lie down on her back on the bed as climbed on top of her, swiftly plunging his fullness deep inside, with a rapid deliberation that she loved, until Rich, too, came, and the three lay in unified and satisfied silence.

Deidre chuckled to herself, noting the sheets and bedding to be in complete disarray and damp from both the sweat and juices of the trio, but she didn't care. No one did, as three lay exhausted in varying positions on the bed. There would be nothing taboo that night, or any of the glorious nights to follow, and there were no complaints either.

Feeling exhausted and tranquil, Mark suggested that they should get into the hot tub before going to sleep. Both Deidre and Rich agreed, each knowing there would be more fun in the hot tub before surrendering to a coma-like like sleep state very soon.

The warm water pulsating on Deidre's skin felt good as she leaned her back into the cushioned wall of the hot tub and closed her eyes in serenity of the moment. It certainly was fortunate for me that Sandra became occupied elsewhere! Deidre deduced with jubilance, as she would have both Mark and Rich all to herself.

Both men lowered themselves into the hot tub and began working their way toward Deidre. The sexually driven water activities rivaled the bedroom action, leaving all three playmates completely spent and ready to sleep for the night—or so it seemed at that moment.

After rinsing herself off, Deidre crawled into the middle of the bed, looking forward to some rest, with Mark to her left and Rich to her right. Mark was still feeling frisky but, like Deidre, he was clearly ready for some shut-eye first. Rich, on the other hand, was nowhere near done with Deidre just yet. Though half asleep, Deidre could feel Rich's hard penis against her leg, and there would be no ignoring it. Turning to face Rich, she could see a broad and mischievous smile in the dimly lit room.

"Roll over onto your stomach," Rich ordered Deidre, with a whisper in her ear. Knowing exactly what position Rich had in mind and liking it, Deidre complied in eager anticipation of being mounted from behind, a favorite because he could enter so deeply that she would surely come at least once more. Deidre, now propped up on her hands and knees, could feel Rich's hugeness entering her forcefully and slowly withdrawing. As he held on tightly to her waist, he picked up speed, and although she felt his action was somewhat rough, she certainly didn't mind! So few men she had encountered had ever taken the upper hand with her in the bedroom, which she believed to be due to her alpha personality. She was really going to enjoy this.

The writhing action of the two would go unnoticed by Mark, sleeping nearby, until Rich and Deidre had migrated across the sheets in their passionate dance. Waking up enough to realize what he was missing out on, Mark could feel Deidre's hand caressing his cock, arousing him to full attention, much to her delight. This is heavenly! Deidre thought to herself, hearing Rich moaning in pleasure from behind her as his body shuddered. Releasing himself into her, he collapsed on the bed next to her once again.

Deidre now focused on Mark and his re-energized lust for

her. Mark and Deidre contorted themselves in and out of sexual positions in their desire-driven jockeying, reaching contentment once more.

In less than one hour, the satisfied trio lay silently, sprawled out on the bed in varying positions, too exhausted to move, for what seemed like an eternity. They would finally work their way up to the top of the bed, climbing under the covers and spooning each other, for some much-needed sleep or until the next go-around.

Wow, did I ever fall asleep hard and fast that night! Deidre reminisced, sipping her cocktail in satisfaction with a smile. Her two new lovers would become additions to her "friends with benefits list," she told herself. Deidre had wound up spending a total of three nights and four days with her new friends, with the days spent out on the water in Mark's large boat, with all three naked. The two men would freely initiate sex with Deidre, each at any given moment. Every night the trio would get dinner out of the way before another evening of steamy hot tub action, followed up with more hard-core sex in which no position was taboo.

On the fourth evening, Deidre remembered, she had become annoyed with Mark, who would become very opinionated about topics under discussion at various times when the three were not in the throes of a sexual session.

Deidre's passion in the bedroom could be rivaled only by her anger when an unnecessary jab or insult was thrown at her, as the two men soon found out. Mark carelessly blurted out an offensive remark on their final night together, oblivious to its ramifications. And so, with no more discussion or sex necessary as far as Deidre was concerned, she stood up and put her clothes back on, much to the amazement and dismay of both Mark and Rich. She loathed Mark at that very moment. Deidre had shared her body willingly and enjoyably with both Mark and Rich, but neither would ever see inside her heart, she realized while leaving

Mark's house that night.

So now for the dilemma, Deidre contemplated while sipping a cocktail of tears, cranberry, and vodka, in the ensuing darkness visible from her small screened-in porch. Mark had been nice for the most part, and had even called the next morning and apologized, but she knew beyond the several additional dates they would have that he was only wanting sex. But then again, how was I any different?! Deidre chuckled to herself. After all, I was the only female with two men. Who made out better in that deal? She rationalized without shame, as a knowing smile came across her face, erasing the bitterness she had felt just moments earlier.

But just sitting out on the porch reminiscing was not going to satisfy the immediate craving at hand, Deidre knew. Looking down to see her drinking glass was now empty, Deidre set off to the kitchen to make herself another cocktail as she finalized her plan for that night's action.

With a fresh drink in hand, Deidre walked over to queue up some old familiar music on her stereo, A sultry, sexy song is just what I need to hear right now, she thought.

Within moments, the sound of an old familiar voice began to sensually fill the room. "Come Away with Me," by Nora Jones, was a favorite of Deidre's, bringing back bittersweet memories of a previous lover, someone she had had serious feelings for several years earlier, but who was no longer in her life.

Placing her drink down on the coffee table, Deidre wrapped her arms around herself, as if to give herself a hug, as she reminisced about his hug, and how much she wished she could hold him in her arms just once again, while swaying back and forth in time to the soft music.

The lyric about listening to the rain while being safe in a lover's arms brought back wonderfully painful memories, taunting Deidre with a man she loved but knew she could never have.

That seemed to always be the story in her love life: The timing was never right for one reason or another.

But Deidre's soulful dance of depression would be interrupted by the distinctive ring tone of her psychology practice's answering service, causing immediate concern. Deidre's mind immediately flipped the memory switch to "off," knowing she was not on call this weekend and would only have been called for something important, something she had to take care of personally or needed to be made aware of.

"Hello?" Deidre asked with anticipatory concern.

"Dr. Villanova?" the familiar voice queried.

"Hi, Olivia," Deidre said. "What's up? You know that I'm not on call this weekend unless it's something important. You should be calling Dr. Sharp," Deidre said with concerned annoyance. I need this weekend so badly or I will lose my sanity, Deidre thought to herself.

"No, Dr. Villanova, nothing's wrong. I'm actually calling to give you some important good news!" Olivia said quickly with a light chuckle, attempting to dissuade any further stressful thoughts that Deidre had at that time.

Relaxing somewhat now, Deidre breathed a heavy sigh of relief and asked, "So, what's the news?"

Olivia began to explain. "I just received a call from the mother of a patient of yours by the name of Katrina Moss. She just wanted you to know that Katrina and her baby are both safe and sound back at home. Her mom also said that she would be contacting you on Tuesday, with further details, but not to worry."

"Thank you so much, Olivia!" Deidre responded in relief at hearing the good news, and for being pulled out of her previous heavy-hearted despair. "Have a great weekend, and thank you, Olivia!"

"You too, Dr. Villanova. I promise not to bother you again on your weekend off!" Olivia finished.

"No problem, Olivia. Take care," Deidre said, while reaching down to pick up her drink and return her thoughts to the immediate need at hand, a plan for the night.

Deidre headed off to shower and start getting ready. The warm water felt so good against her tense muscles as she stood with her back to the pulsating stream, allowing it to jet onto just the right areas of her neck and shoulders.

Having been sidetracked earlier by her erotic reminiscence and the phone call, Deidre knew the night was rapidly escaping her. It was already nearly nine o'clock. This will be a quick night, she surmised in an attempt to salvage what was left of it, and realized Jerry to be the perfect boy toy for a night like this — absolutely perfect.

Chapter 2
Jerry

My parents would absolutely die if they knew about these things I do! Deidre thought to herself, laughing out loud, as she accessed her cell phone's contact list in search of Jerry's number. Deidre had devised a clever manner in which to catalogue or categorize her playmates, so that only she could access the grouping. When a new name and number was to be added to the "friends with benefits" list, Deidre would enter the first and last name as usual; however, where there was an optional line to enter a "Company Name," she would enter the letters "BTX." Having labeled each of her boy toys listings with BTX, she needed only to enter "BTX" in the search box to discreetly pull up her entire list of options for any occasion, with no one else aware of what the letters associated with her "special friends" meant. If someone became curious as to an incoming call or text, Deidre would explain it away as some sort of business association, squelching any further inquiries.

Here I am, an Ivy League graduate, making a booty call to someone young enough to be my son! Deidre pondered in amusement with an impish smirk, feeling no shame whatsoever

"Hey there, handsome—what you up to tonight?" Deidre asked Jerry, hopeful that her wild young buck was free for at least a fraction of the night.

"Where you been, babe? I tried calling you a few times and left several messages, but you never answered them. Thought you'd either dropped off the face of the earth or found someone to replace me, kitten. You're not mad at me, are you?"

"I'm sorry, Jerry. Been crazy busy with work and life, but I finally have the whole weekend off and was really hoping you were free to come over tonight, even if it's for just a little while. I desperately need to see you, Jerry—I've been so horny. I miss you so much! Any chance you could stop over?"

"So you're missing me, are you, kitten?!" Jerry asked in a tone dripping with seductive sarcasm. "I've had a long workday myself and just got home—haven't even showered yet. I'm a sweaty mess, but not from you this time! But I could make it to your place in probably an hour. About eight-thirty sound fast enough for you?"

A wicked smile fueled by erotic thoughts crossed Deidre's face as she answered, "Sounds like a plan. I'll be waiting with bated breath, and you can plan on getting sweaty again when I get through with you!" Every erogenous zone in her body was now aroused, awakened, and eagerly awaiting her young stallion's attention.

"Then I'll see you soon, kitten! Be ready for some serious fun!" Jerry instructed her playfully.

"Oh, I am! I'll see you soon!" Deidre exclaimed with excitement, before hanging up the phone.

Already showered, Deidre quickly dabbed on some of her favorite musky perfume before slipping into a sexy black mesh negligée with pink silk insets, Jerry's favorite one, though she thought it to be a waste of time as it would be removed within the first few minutes anyway. She studied herself in the mirror to make certain that no important details had been overlooked.

"Oh damn! I forgot the lipstick!" Deidre blurted aloud while grabbing the sweet-tasting clear lip gloss from her drawer and rolling it on. Taking a last approving glance at herself, Deidre smiled, feeling her appearance to be totally complete for her special visitor's arrival.

With only a few moments remaining to prepare for Jerry's arrival, Deidre hurriedly scanned the house, picking up some haphazardly thrown clothes and shoes, before lighting several strategically placed candles throughout the living room and bedroom, helping to set the mood for the arrival of her boy toy.

Deidre lay on the living room sofa, soaking in total relaxation for a moment. Everything seemed to be perfectly in place, she thought to herself, as sultry sounds snaked through the room, and ambient candle flames flickered, dancing wildly about the room and the ceiling as if in preparation for enjoyment of the upcoming activities they would help to enhance.

At just thirty-three years of age, Jerry was not Deidre's greenest playmate, but he was certainly charged with a boundless youthful sexual energy and appetite, which she appreciated and utilized to full advantage.

Hearing a loud knock, knock, knock, on the door, Deidre leapt from the couch, glancing briefly in the foyer mirror before opening the front door. Absolutely perfect! She reasoned to herself.

Opening the door, Deidre stood admiringly examining the blossoming and bright-eyed beau standing in front of her now, with a boyishly beautiful and mischievous grin, beaming from ear to ear.

"Get in here now!" Deidre ordered in a sexy growl, her senses heightening as she grabbed his hand, pulling him inside, and then closing the door to the rest of the world.

Deidre loved the fact that Jerry was tall. At nearly six-foot three, he had a well-defined, statuesque, and Herculean physique, which was complemented by shoulder-length curly black hair, green eyes, and perfectly white teeth.

In spite of Jerry's tender young age, he was the perfect blend of an old seasoned soul, eager to please his woman instead of just satisfying himself, with the strength and stamina of youth, allowing for repeat performances that sometimes lasted effortlessly all night.

Jerry would often become frustrated with Deidre when she insisted that theirs was solely a relationship of sex. No matter how she broke it down for him and tried to explain it, Jerry was unrelenting in his attempts to persuade Deidre that the enormous age difference between them was irrelevant, but Deidre knew better.

And while the sexual interconnection between them might have been unquestionably epic, more than satisfying one vital component, Deidre felt he lacked the second most vital component of a lasting relationship. Jerry simply had not experienced enough of life yet to arrest her psychologically highbrow interests, regardless of how efficiently he employed the use of fuzzy handcuffs to arrest her sexual interest in the bedroom.

Deidre realized that Jerry was confusing her insatiable sexual appetite with the basis of a long-lasting relationship, and she didn't want to hurt this tender and ethereal soul. Deidre realized Jerry's future potential and value to females, who stood to benefit from his passion, fire, and bedroom talents.

Within minutes, the venereally fraught duo would be naked, making their way to the bedroom without further conversation or thought necessary.

Upon entering the bedroom, very much alive with dancing candlelight as well, Deidre laughed to herself at the thought that she needed to reinforce the bedframe prior to Jerry's next visit, lest it collapse on the floor. But that won't stop the activities I have planned for you for tonight, baby, Deidre knew that for sure.

His favorite position was missionary, so when Jerry instructed Deidre to "assume the position," she knew just what position to get in. She not only loved it but expected and wanted it as well.

Deidre indulged herself in thought about the pounding she knew she would be experiencing very soon. But tonight she wanted to turn the tables just a bit, taking the upper hand for a while first.

"Lie on your back, Jerry," Deidre said softly, fully aware that he was expecting to mount her instead. As Deidre amorously observed the gorgeous young man lying in front of her, she stared into his eyes momentarily before panning down his chest and rock-hard abdomen, to see a most inviting and stiff cock thrusting out just below, eagerly awaiting further attention.

"Lie very, very still, baby," Deidre instructed, as sensual music filled the room and the soft candle flames continued with their own hedonistic dance, freely and brilliantly jumping from wall to wall in their own uniquely wild celebration.

Slowly straddling Jerry's lower legs on her hands and knees, Deidre began to teasingly kiss and gently lick Jerry's inner thighs. Deidre so enjoyed seeing Jerry struggling to remain composed and compliant with her instruction to lie still, beneath the pleasurable and welcoming erotic torture, which she was meting out to him at that moment.

"No, no, no—you mustn't move, Jerry!" Deidre corrected him with an evil smile, making him aware that there would be more to come—much more to come.

Placing her hands gently on his thighs for balance, Deidre then lowered her mouth to lick his balls gently, one at a time, observing his rigid penis involuntarily respond to the sensation she was eliciting.

Realizing the effect this was having on Jerry, Deidre continued her torment on Jerry even further, gently sucking each ball, with her tongue reaching out underneath to even farther nether regions. Jerry's body jerked and shook under the pressure. He was unable to lie still any longer, and his pelvis began writhing in a circular motion under the assault, as if begging for more.

With her plan wildly in motion now, Deidre was finding it increasingly difficult to refrain from jumping on top of him. She strongly desired to feel him inside her, but she continued on her deliciously torturous course.

In order to really drive Jerry crazy, Deidre pressed her tongue into the soft spot where the underside of the penis meets the scrotum, pressing inward and then teasingly up and down. She gently licked the underside of his shaft, all the while delighting in hearing Jerry's loud moans. It pleased her that he was now tightly clenching the pillow between his fists, appearing barely able to survive Deidre's frolicsome ways for much longer.

Sensing that the end was now near, Deidre lowered her mouth on his tip, running her tongue around its rim, and then, without warning, she took him completely down her throat, not an easy task when Jerry was this granite hard. Deidre loved knowing that she was causing her young lover to nearly come unglued.

Visibly flustered now, Jerry wasn't able to bear another moment of Deidre's sexual assault on him, and he suddenly reached up and grabbed Deidre's head, demanding her, "Stop," in a firm tone, which she knew she needed to obey.

The seriously intent expression on Jerry's face and look in his eyes alerted Deidre that she was really in for it now. As Jerry abruptly sat up, he forcefully pulled her up onto him with ease and determination. Deidre found herself in one of her favorite positions once again, and took full advantage of every inch of her musclebound beauty, lowering herself down on his hard cock, which now twitched, until she came to rest on his pelvis, in complete and utter ecstasy.

"You feel so damn good!" Deidre decried aloud, as she slid herself up and down on him in a slow rhythm, wanting to feel and enjoy every ridge and vein, and especially his bulbous tip, while Jerry lifted his pelvis up to meet her, accommodating and complementing each of Deidre's movements, which became increasingly more rapid with each deeper thrust. With Jerry's passionate and surreal strength, Deidre found these sessions of unbridled erotica to be painfully amazing, something she had never experienced with anyone else.

In retrospect, Deidre often wondered how she was able to tolerate such savage encounters when they lasted all night long. "Holy shit! I'm going to need time to recover from this one," Deidre informed herself in utmost pleasure.

Jerry was now holding on tightly to Deidre's waist, keeping her pelvis elevated slightly off him, as he drove himself into her faster and faster, until both he and Deidre orgasmed fiercely and simultaneously.

Deidre, completely exhausted now, slowly dismounted from Jerry and lay down next to him, feeling his body sweat and heart race with her hand on his chest.

"Wow, kitten. That was fucking amazing!" Jerry exclaimed with a smile, as he pulled her in close to him with a hug. Deidre closed her eyes and lay still, relishing the moment and enjoying the calm serenity she felt, while music continued softly in the background. Deidre loved how Jerry would wear her out so, making her forget any and all stressors she had been concerned with prior to his visits each time.

In fact, Jerry repeated his pleasurable assaults on Deidre at least several times during each of the nights he spent with her, and this night would be no different, she knew. She also realized any peaceful rest would be a brief one, as this had only been Round One for the night.

But as Deidre began to drift off into a light sleep, she suddenly became aware of the candles, which she had left burning during their evening, and she knew she needed to blow them out to prevent a fire. Getting off the bed slowly, so as not to break the tranquil mood, Deidre slipped into the living room first and extinguished the still-dancing flames, allowing the soft music to continue.

Upon returning to the bedroom, Deidre leaned over to blow out one of the sweet-smelling candles on the dresser but was stopped by Jerry's sleepy voice: "Not so fast, Princess. I'm not through with you just yet!"

Deidre turned to look at Jerry, who was lying gloriously bare on the bed, with no covers hiding his wonderful nakedness. And with a weary yet wanton smile, Deidre returned to the disheveled bed, leaving the bedroom to remain aglow in sweet-smelling candlelight and sexual satiation. As Deidre lay down next to Jerry, he said "Roll over," looking at her intently.

Deidre knew that "Roll over" meant she was to get on her

27

hands and knees, with her upper body resting face-down on a pillow. Deidre's backside would stick upward, a position she had become very practiced at and proficient with.

With Deidre now in position, Jerry approached her from behind, with his cock hard and ready. First feeling inside her for moisture with his fingers, he began slowly sliding himself into her. Deidre could feel Jerry's strong hands gripping her hips. She loved feeling him in her like this and could tell by his firm grasp that this round would be as powerful as the rest.

"Please start out slowly, Jerry," Deidre plead playfully, loving how his cock felt as he could tease her to near orgasm, just by sliding the head of his cock in and out of her slowly. But while Deidre would slip into a trance-like state during this time, Jerry could keep up such a slow rhythm for more than just a few minutes before he began to slam himself into her, with an increasing speed that she would liken to that of a jackrabbit.

Once Jerry's speed and force of thrust had reached their peak, Deidre would lose any ability to keep from squirting, soon saturating the bed, and that was exactly what turned Jerry on about her. Deidre found it nearly impossible to remain in place when Jerry got to this point, often feeling her head being driven up to the headboard. She would attempt to scoot herself backward without breaking stride, which would only make Jerry's impact even deeper.

"That's it! That's it! I'm coming now, babe!" Jerry cried out loudly, deeply thrusting himself into her one final time and then freezing in position as he released himself. The feel of him filling her prompted Deidre to have her own fabulous G-spot orgasm this time, and she screamed out "Yes! Yes!" as her entire body quivered in delight.

The pair remained completely still, locked together in a most special moment of ecstasy, with neither one anxious to break the blissful euphoria they each felt. But Deidre knew that the bedding would have to be changed, before they could lie back down again, and she was now ready for some serious shut-eye. Slowly crawling off the bed, Deidre made her way into the bathroom to clean up, feeling her legs to be a bit shaky from having been splayed open during the pummeling she had just received. She made sure not to slip getting into the shower, with Jerry coming in to join her to clean off as well.

Now showered, clean and dried off, Deidre fetched a set of fresh sheets from the closet and turned on a small bedside lamp. She could see that the entire bed was now re-located several feet away from the wall, which it was normally pushed against, the spot in which it had been located just prior to the activities.

"Oh my God, look at the bed, Jerry!" Deidre exclaimed with laughter. Jerry was just returning from the bathroom, still towel-drying his hair. "Again, really?!" she said, as they both began to laugh and move the bed back to its original position before going to sleep for the night. I fucking love these moments, Deidre thought, knowing that no one would ever believe her if she told them about this, although she knew she could never, ever tell a single soul. This part of her life had to be kept well hidden from the others in her world both personally and professionally. People would quickly pass judgment on her actions, either due to not understanding her voracious sexual appetite, or due to bitterness in that they were not having as much fun as she was. Most often, Deidre believed, it was because they lacked the surreal sex life that she enjoyed on a regular basis.

With the bed now somewhat back in its place and clean sheets on it, Deidre quickly blew out the dancing candles in the bedroom and then climbed under the covers to snuggle with Jerry, until the early morning hours, when she knew he would very often be ready for more play.

Having been worked out to exhaustion during the evening with Jerry, Deidre slept soundly throughout the remainder of the night. She woke the next morning to find herself on the other side of the bed from Jerry, fully stretched out as the sun peeked in thru the bedroom window, waking her up. Glancing across the bed, she could see that Jerry remained fast asleep and seemingly unfazed by the sun's intrusion. She had slept so hard during the night that she did not remember moving from Jerry's stronghold, and she was happy that her sleep had been uninterrupted this time.

The smell of fresh coffee brewing waifed into the bedroom, letting Deidre know it was seven o'clock, the time she had set it for auto-brew. Now to get Jerry up from hibernation, she thought to herself, knowing he would sleep in for hours if she let him, or until he wanted to start up again, but she had things to do today. There was not the time to get things started up again this morning Deidre knew, appreciating that she felt so good since having gotten so much uninterrupted sleep during the night.

"Hey, handsome," she said after rolling over on her side to face Jerry, who was sleeping like a baby. "It's time to get up, sleepyhead. Coffee's ready," Deidre announced as she crept off the bed, and then set out to the kitchen to get them both a cup of joe. She always enjoyed sitting on the back porch to relax in the morning. She needed to get Jerry out of the bedroom before he wanted to start playing around again, and to have some small talk with him before getting him on his way.

Jerry came to meet Deidre on the outside porch with only his briefs covering the pertinent area. Wow! she thought to herself, looking at her young lover's perfectly fit physique, now illuminated by the sun which shone from behind him. Jerry yawned sleepily as he staggered out and sat down in a chair next to her.

"Here you go," Deidre said, handing Jerry his cup of coffee and then sipping on her own. "I'm going to need to get going soon," she said, awaiting his reaction and knowing he would not be happy about it.

"So, what are your plans for tonight?" Jerry asked, yawning as he struggled with the sunlight quickly coming in full force, causing him to move his chair in order to keep the unwelcomed light from glaring in his eyes.

"Not sure yet," she answered. "I'm supposed to go to a dinner party tonight, but if I don't I can give you a call if you'd like."

There was no dinner party planned, but Deidre felt the need to give herself an "out" with Jerry. This was the hardest part with him—cutting him loose and getting him to leave in the morning. It was also one reason she hesitated in inviting him over at times. But finally, it would be the main reason she knew she needed to cut him off, and let him go. This was not the right moment, however; it would have to wait.

"I have a job I need to check on this afternoon, but it isn't going to take too long," Jerry answered as he sat back, relaxing in the chair and enjoying his coffee. "I could easily stop back by when I'm done."

Aaahh, here he goes, Deidre realized. He would want to be with her for the entire weekend, she knew. The air with which Jerry sat and made eye contact with her had become increasingly worrisome.

What if I encounter him while I'm out and about? she contemplated, concerned with what his reaction might be. He was a very passionate and fiery soul, and he was never going to accept the reality of the situation, no matter how many times she explained it to him.

I'm really playing with fire now! she thought to herself uncomfortably at that moment, as her cell phone began to chime, alerting her that an incoming text had arrived.

Not eager to incite Jerry's quick suspicions, Deidre disregarded the text with a hand wave, reiterating the fact that she was off duty for the weekend, but in fact she knew the chime's unique and melodic meaning, and it took everything within her not to run for her phone at that moment.

The text tone was a carefully selected one. It was a well-known song, from a famous rock band, which one of her most secret of lovers performed in. She had not heard from Roger, a very special lover and coveted listing in her "BTX" list, for some time. Roger was very good at rocking her world each and every time they got together.

Nearly unable to contain herself, hearing the text alert a second time, Deidre could no longer concentrate on her conversation with Jerry, and the expression on his face told her that he was keenly observant beyond his tender years.

"Look, Jerry, I am going to need to address that text soon. I can't imagine why they are bothering me on my day off, but it could be important," Deidre nonchalantly briefed, hoping to allay Jerry's obvious suspicions.

Deidre sensed a definite change in the tone of their morning's discussion, and after offering Jerry a refill on his coffee, she told him she needed to jump in the shower in a few minutes, preparing him to be politely escorted out of the house.

"So you'll definitely call me if you don't go tonight?" Jerry inquired, with the sound of apparent skepticism.

"I absolutely will, Jerry, I love having you over, but I still have things I need to do. And I really should go to the dinner party. These are good friends of mine who I haven't seen in a long time, and surely you must have some young 'chickie' to have fun with tonight!" she said in a lighthearted and joking manner, yet with the intention of driving home a message to him.

"You know how I feel about that topic, Deidre," Jerry retorted sarcastically as he rose to his feet and now stood staring intently into her face.

Wanting nothing more than to pull his briefs down one more time, she figured it was better not to. I can't fuel this fire anymore this morning, Deidre thought to herself standing up to meet him face to his shoulders.

Deidre then reached up to Jerry's neck and pulled his face toward her, giving him a quick kiss on the lips.

"I'll give you a call later," she said and turned on her heel to head for the shower.

"Okay, kitten, I got the message," Jerry said as he retreated to the bedroom to put his clothes on.

Deidre had already stepped into the shower as Jerry was getting dressed, and she stood enjoying the warm water running down her tired body, as she was in deep thought as to how she needed to handle Jerry.

"Later, babe," she heard Jerry say as he peeked his head in the bathroom before leaving. "Have a good one, Jerry," Deidre answered as she reached for her shampoo, knowing her hair was a complete disaster after the previous night's workout.

Feeling a sense of relief after hearing the front door close, knowing that Jerry had gone, Deidre cautioned herself once again I am going to have to end this soon! She let out a heavy sigh and returned her thoughts to the healing warmth of the water, allowing it to wash away any and all of her cares for the moment.

Chapter 3
A Flaming Hot Birthday Party

Deidre was much more relaxed since showering. It also helped to know that Jerry had finally left without the drama that usually accompanied these morning leave-takings. She could now get on with her day. First things first, she thought to herself while reaching for her cell phone to retrieve Roger's text to read:

Long time no see. We will be playing a gig not too far from you just before Christmas. I will get in touch with you as soon as I have a confirmed schedule. Maybe we can hook up. I would really love to see you… and do other things to you!

Elated after having read Roger's text, Deidre responded with "I can't wait! But I will come see you only if I get a private performance of my very own!"

"Oh you can bet on it, sexy! Ttyl," Roger replied.

Deidre finished the conversation by sending an icon of a cartoon character blowing a kiss.

The text messages from Roger were exactly what Deidre needed to distract her from her thoughts concerning Jerry.

What a great way to start a beautiful Saturday morning, Deidre thought dreamily as she headed to her bedroom to get dressed for her morning's gym workout. She really did not feel the need for any additional exercise after the intense workout she had gotten with Jerry the previous night, but Deidre knew all too well that her mental health relied on it and the endorphin release it brought about.

Just before Deidre could make it out the door, her phone rang. It was her friend Camille, who wanted to know if she would come to a surprise birthday party over the weekend for Deborah, a mutual friend, who was turning fifty years old. "I'm sorry about the short notice. We planned this at the last minute, and I sure hope you can make it. It's been forever since we've all gotten together, way too long. I hope you can make it tonight, Deidre, even for just a little while," Camille pleaded.

Deidre knew Deborah well and did not care much for her, feeling her to be catty and a bit of a snob. And while Deidre enjoyed the finer things in life, she couldn't stand being around people who were petty, pretentious, and judgmental. Making sure that those around you know what you have had never been important to Deidre, but she did miss Camille, and a few others who Camille said would be there, so she said, "Sure. That sounds like fun. Where are we meeting?" Deidre asked.

"At that nightclub A Twisted Joint."

It was appropriately named, Deidre felt, knowing that some of her most "twisted" friends and a few of her colleagues were frequent patrons. In the middle of all the nightlife downtown, A Twisted Joint always had great music and dancing, something Deidre adored doing. She could get totally lost in dancing for hours, no matter who she was with, if the music and vibes were good.

After getting in a good workout at the gym, Deidre stopped off at her favorite lunch spot for a salad before heading home to get some work done around the house.

I can't wait to see Roger again, Deidre thought excitedly while tidying up the house and catching up on laundry from the previous work week. She then headed to the bedroom to get things back in order in there after the wild activities from the night before, which always created additional laundry and cleaning.

While reaching to collect the dirty sheets from the hamper, Deidre realized that the bed was still not entirely back in its place and began to chuckle, as she remembered the wild night she and Jerry had just enjoyed. Deidre gloried in the raucous sessions with Jerry, never thinking twice about the clean-up afterward. The only negative aftertaste came from the fact that Jerry would always pressure her, wanting a relationship, something that could not and would not ever happen. But she knew she would never forget their torrid nights together.

The afternoon hours slipped by quickly as Deidre kept busy with her chores. It occurred to her that she had not heard from her friend Gregory yet, to confirm their date for the next afternoon. Dr. Gregory George was a well-respected colleague of Deidre's, whom she also had become very good friends with over the past fifteen years, while they had been working together. Gregory had become not only a cherished friend but was also a confidant of Deidre's, someone she could tell anything to and could call at any time of the day or night.

"Even the best of psychologists need someone that they can talk to on occasion," Deidre had often informed her friends and colleagues. But not everyone is willing to admit that they need help, she knew. Most were afraid it showed a sign of weakness, but Deidre felt it necessary to decompress from her stressful and sometimes overwhelming job. She knew that having an invaluable friend like Gregory enabled her to function at peak performance level.

With all of her work done, it was now nearing five o'clock in the afternoon, and Deidre realized that she needed to start getting ready for her evening out with her friends, many of whom she had not seen in some time. She was looking forward to going out with Camille and the others, and not having to stress out over a date tonight.

Deidre knew that the nightclub they were going to have a reputation as a "meat market," where men and women went when they were in need of a hook-up. Deidre was not at all interested in seeking out a suitor for the night, but she was looking forward to busting loose on the dance floor with her friends and getting lost in the music. She also felt an element of comfort in knowing that this particular nightclub was located quite a distance from her practice. The last thing she wanted or needed was to run into any of her patients while she was out partying.

From previous visits to the club, Deidre remembered that

everyone dressed lively, and she wanted to be eye-catching. I do believe that tonight's the night to break out my short denim skirt, Deidre thought to herself, removing it from a hanger in the closet. Hmmm… But which top should I dress this up with? She carefully eyed her selection of sexy bustiers in a range of styles and colors.

Oh yes, this one will be perfect for the evening! She removed an expensive, hand-beaded ivory-colored corset from its special hanger and laid it out on her bed. This was one of Deidre's favorites. She was always amazed that, no matter what activities she was engaged in, it managed to not only stay up but hold her breasts in as well.

As she began studying her vast assortment of shoes in search of the perfect pair to complement her clothes for the evening, Deidre realized that the clothes and shoes had to not only be sexy, but be ones that she could dance in for hours. She was never one to dress very conservatively, except at work and its associated meetings, unless she absolutely had to. And tonight was definitely not a night that she needed, or cared, to be conservative. She was looking to have an enjoyable, worry-free night.

Once she had gotten ready and felt dressed-to-kill, Deidre drove to the club to meet her friends. Everyone had arrived early as they had been instructed, in order to surprise Deborah, the birthday girl, when she walked in the door. And she certainly was surprised. After several drinks, introductions, and other pleasantries had been exchanged, they sang "Happy Birthday," after which Camille and several others headed to the dance floor to get things started for the night, with Deidre quick to join in.

This will be an early night for me, Deidre thought, feeling somewhat weary from her intense sexual workout with Jerry the previous night, and then her gym workout earlier in the day. But the music was invitingly perfect for dancing, and so was the milieu, causing Deidre to stay longer than she had planned to. Unwilling to let the good times come to an end, Deidre danced non-stop through song after song, realizing she was now sweating, and figured she should return to the table with the rest of the group, once the current song had finished.

But as the song was winding to a close, Deidre glanced across the dance floor to see a very handsome man dancing wildly erotically with a woman. Still moving her body in rhythm to the music, Deidre found herself distracted by how well the man moved on the dance floor. What an absolutely gorgeous free spirit, she thought. As Deidre danced, she could not help glancing over intermittently to watch the sexy stranger, and found herself imagining how exciting his bedroom moves must be. What a very pleasurable distraction, she thought, realizing she was preoccupied by his body's sensual movement.

Though sweating, and despite having felt so tired just moments earlier, Deidre now felt rejuvenated and energized as she continued to dance. Her curiosity-piqued desire caused her to discreetly peek the stranger's way often, wishing he were alone. Just one more song, Deidre told herself, looking over to notice that the handsome stranger was now peering her way in an inviting manner. He navigated his way around the dance floor with amazing ease and sex appeal, almost as if he was sending a message to her. His pelvis gyrated in perfect timing to the music so naturally, she felt.

The handsome stranger was tall and lean, with glowing shoulder-length, light golden-brown wavy hair. Although she couldn't tell where he was from, he had a very exotic look about him, something she found exceedingly attractive. Deidre had always found men of this type to be amazing lovers.

Holy shit! Where the fuck did you come from?! I could jump you in a minute! She fantasized dreamily, then quickly reoriented herself to the fact that he was with someone else. Deidre decided to finally leave the dance floor and sit down with her friends back at the table for a quick rest and a drink to cool off. She made sure to sit in a seat at the table from which she could still catch a glimpse of her new interest, thinking nothing would ever come of it. Within a few minutes Deidre turned her back to the delicious dancing man, becoming engrossed in conversation with her friends at the table and forgetting the man.

But although Deidre's back might have been deliberately turned to discontinue her torturous temptation, out of the corner of her eye she could see the seductive stranger coming toward her table with a smile on his face, and she froze wondering why he was coming in that direction. Deidre felt like her world was in slow-motion and tried desperately to appear nonchalant as he approached. She couldn't concentrate on any of the jokes or conversation at the table during those gripping moments, which put Deidre in a euphoric, fog-like state.

As the sexy stranger slowly approached the table, Deidre immediately became aroused by his sweet-smelling cologne invading her nostrils. Once beside her table, the handsome stranger peered over to meet Deidre's eyes, then gave her an approving nod—or was it an inviting nod?—leaving Deidre feeling good but a bit confused. She wasn't sure of the message he was sending, but with the way he intently stared, she believed he meant his look to come across as an invitation. What does he want? Deidre pondered.

Deidre realized that the stranger was heading toward the back of the club, where there was a smaller, more intimate bar, with a dark hallway leading to the bathrooms a bit farther away.

Maybe he wants me to join him at the back bar for a drink, she thought, feeling excitement mounting between her thighs and tingling in her nipples. Worst case scenario, I can simply go back and use the restroom, if I've read too much into his flirting, she assured herself while grabbing her purse and momentarily excusing herself from the group. She definitely didn't want to let this opportunity escape her.

Approaching the dimly lit bar in the back, Deidre quickly looked around to see if the handsome stranger might be there waiting for her, but he was nowhere to be seen. Fuck! I must have misinterpreted that message! Deidre thought disappointedly.

Now feeling a little awkward about the situation, she wondered if, in fact, the man had only been giving her an approving gesture rather than an inviting one. Well, I guess it's time for plan B, she instructed herself. I'll hit the restroom and comb my hair. She began walking to the very back wall of the club, where the restrooms were located.

They were situated at the end of a long, angled hallway, which could not be seen until you took a quick left turn down a smaller walkway. The area was always poorly lit, making Deidre a little uneasy. She was somewhat relieved to see the illuminated fluorescent restroom signs, glowing in the distance as she was making her way down the long, dark walk. But just as she felt relief, a hand reached out and gently grabbed her left arm, pulling her into the shadows off to the side of the hallway.

Deidre had been caught off guard, yet strangely she wasn't afraid. She turned in the direction she was being pulled toward now and could just barely see the golden-brown hair of the handsome man in the shadows. She also recognized his inviting cologne. Every hair on her body stood on end at that moment, as Deidre felt overwhelming excitement, mixed with enticing intrigue, racing through her mind and body.

"Oh my God, you scared the shit out of me!" Deidre smiled as she boldly scolded her stranger.

A broad and disarming smile came across the handsome stranger's face in return as he turned now to face her, towering over her in a moment that Deidre found to be quite sensual.

"I just had to meet you," he said as he handed her a small yellow piece of paper with his name and phone number. Deidre was not able to read what it said, due to the poor lighting, so she fastidiously tucked the note into the pocket of her jean skirt for safekeeping.

"My name is Carlo," the man said. His voice had a beautiful accent she couldn't identify. He placed his hands gently on her shoulders, showing no sign of threat whatsoever.

Deidre, sensing no harm from the very sexy and erotic man, stood speechless, staring at him in total disbelief not only of the situation but of what she was feeling for him at that moment. This is absolutely crazy, Deidre thought. How in the living hell do I get into these weird situations? she wondered in amazement.

"Well, Carlo, I must say you are one hell of a handsome man, as well as a very sexy dancer!" she said with an impish grin. "My name is Deidre. But didn't I just see you on the dance floor with another woman?"

Through some light laughter, Carlo replied, "Yes, that is an old girlfriend. We are really just friends now, and I stay at her place occasionally when my work brings me into town."

Deidre could sense that Carlo was sincere in what he was saying. "So, she's not a current lover?" she probed further.

"Not at all," Carlo answered calmly.

The energy Deidre could feel coming from Carlo was dizzying. She wanted him to take her right then and there. It was nearly unbearable for Deidre to just stand there staring at Carlo in the shadows, without a word being spoken between them for seconds that seemed so much longer. Lustful thoughts had left Deidre momentarily without words, yet wild thoughts soared through her mind at warp speed.

As Deidre struggled to remain composed as well as to regain her ability to talk, Carlo pulled her tightly into him, and then gently yet forcefully, he grabbed her hair and tilted her head back, and then began erotically kissing her up and down her throat and neck, stopping just shy of her breasts. Uncontrollable shivers raced up and down Deidre's spine each time his moist lips touched her skin. Deidre felt as though she would orgasm right there and then if he continued his assault on her.

But just as suddenly and unexpectedly as Carlo had unleashed his seductive torment on Deidre, he stopped. Now making direct eye contact with Deidre, Carlo said, "You have my number, beautiful lady. Please call me tomorrow. I would like to take you to dinner tomorrow night if that's all right. I want to know who you are!"

Holy shit! Deidre thought. Her heart was pounding as if it wanted to burst out of her chest, and that familiar wanton throbbing was growing stronger between her legs. Did this really just happen?

And then, without warning, Carlo planted a wicked kiss on Deidre's lips. Finally breaking the lip lock, he said, "I truly hope to hear from you," as he turned on his heel and walked back to the action in the club. Deidre, now visibly shaken, made her way into the restroom, feeling the need to have a private moment to absorb what had just happened.

Heading straight to the mirror, Deidre noted her hair to be in severe disarray and pulled a hairbrush from her purse to get her hair back into place, all the while fantasizing about her new friend and soon-to-be lover, Carlo.

Shit! His phone number! she thought to herself while reaching into the pocket of her denim skirt and retrieving the small yellow paper that Carlo had just given her. I can't lose this! she reminded herself as she gazed at the handwriting, finding herself impressed with his penmanship, something most men would not pay much attention to.

She felt his beautiful cursive skill to be an indication that he was somewhat detail oriented and romantic. We'll see about this, Deidre thought skeptically as she stood staring at his note, and then she placed it carefully into a zippered pocket inside her purse for safekeeping.

Feeling a bit calmer and less shaky now, Deidre figured she had better return to her friends at the table, before they started worrying about her and someone came looking for her. Deidre knew that someone was going to make some wisecrack as to where she had gone, and why she was gone so long, and she knew she needed to have a lighthearted answer ready. There was no way she could tell them the truth.

Deidre left the privacy of the restroom, making her way back down the long, dimly lit corridor to the colorful flashing lights and completely packed dance floor. Hearing the band playing "Uptown Funk," by Bruno Mars, had obviously caused many to leave their seats and get loose, with Deidre herself feeling the need to join in, in order to release some of the lust-filled anxiety she now had pent up inside since her encounter with Carlo.

Deidre left her purse at the table and headed straight for the dance floor to join those who were dancing, in hopes that no one would have noticed how long she had been absent. She did not want anybody questioning her at this moment. She just wanted to dance in delight and fantasy right now.

She moved about freely, all the while replaying the event with Carlo over and over again in her mind. She imagined what lovemaking with him would be like, since his earlier and very passionate advance toward her.

If he's anything like that in bed, it will be amazing! Deidre decidedly. She was now sweating again, partly from dancing and partly from the heat she was feeling since her soon-to-be lover had ignited her sexual appetite to a near-frenzied high. Deidre decided to get herself a cocktail and sit with her friends for a while. Arriving at the table, Deidre was surprised to see that Gregory was now sitting at the table with an empty chair next to him, which Deidre slipped into.

"Hey, Gregory, I didn't realize you were going to be here too, or we could have driven together," Deidre said.
"Well, I wasn't sure I would even be able to make it on such short notice, with my crazy schedule," Gregory responded.

"But while I have your attention, and before I forget to ask, are we still on for tomorrow afternoon?" Deidre asked.

"Not only are we still on," Gregory said, "I have a special new wine that I want you to try. It's a delicious blend that I think you will really enjoy."

"I can't wait to speak with you tomorrow," Deidre said, then leaning in closer to Gregory so that no one else in the group could hear her, she said "I have something quite juicy and titillating to tell you about my friend."

"Oh, do tell, Deidre!" Gregory prodded her, intrigued. Deidre could tell that she had sparked his interest as he leaned in closer with eyebrows raised, staring at her, awaiting further explanation.

"Oh, hell no!" Deidre quickly snapped. "There's no way I'm going to discuss this here. Too many ears around. And this, my friend, is not for public consumption," she added with an evil smirk and quick wink.

"Dammit, Deidre! Don't keep me in suspense. You know how much I hate that! You can be so cruel sometimes. Can you at least give me a little hint? Does it involve someone I know, by chance?" Gregory inquired.

Seeing that Gregory's curiosity was piqued, Deidre leaned in even closer to Gregory, to avoid her words from being overheard by anyone else, and then answered "It most certainly does. It involves yours truly and a most interesting and sexually seductive stranger, in a dark hallway right here, tonight."

"Only you, Deidre. I can't wait to hear every sordid detail. Shall we start our cocktail hour around three o'clock tomorrow?" Gregory asked.

"That should allow sufficient time, I do believe," Deidre replied with an affirmative glance and nod. "And now, Gregory, which red wine would you like me to bring a bottle of tomorrow — Ménage à Trois, Château la Companion, or a good old bottle of Ball Buster?" To which they both broke out in laughter.

"Bring whichever suits your fancy, Deidre. I'm sure that

whichever one you bring will be more than adequate," Gregory responded with a chuckle, and then added, "After all, Deidre, once you begin telling me your wild story, I seriously doubt that I'll be focused on the taste of the wine!" That had them both laughing aloud.

The others in the group heard the guffaw between the two, and they began to close in curiously around Deidre and Gregory at the table, prompting the two friends to halt their colorful conversation.

"I'll be at your place around three tomorrow, Gregory. I promise to bring both intrigue and humor to your day!" Deidre finished.

Feeling as though she had been transported directly into the briefest moments of a sexually charged romance novel, Deidre's entire being felt the need to go home now. It was to be a time of solitary erotic reflection combined with thoughts of what future fuckery might be like with Carlo. Deidre felt in need of a powerful fucking, and Carlo had most certainly been the catalyst.

Politely excusing herself from the group, Deidre gave Gregory a big hug and kiss on the cheek and said, "I'll see you tomorrow, my friend." As she turned to leave, she looked back to give Gregory an intriguing backward glance, then exited the club as though she were floating in fog and leaving further elaboration of her surreal encounter with Carlo, the sexy stranger, to dangle intriguingly over Gregory's head.

What an unexpectedly amazing night! This one will definitely be one for the record books! Deidre informed herself laughingly as she drove home to shower and then wrap herself up, first in her bed sheets and then, in the further future fantasies with her soon-to-be new lover, Carlo.

Gregory is going to laugh his ass off when he hears about tonight," Deidre thought.

After arriving home and showering once again, Deidre's mind and body were now enshrouded for a good night's sleep filled with erotica, which filled both her dreams and her corporeal world, unbeknownst to most of those around her.

Oh Gregory dear... You have no clue what fun 411, I have to fill you in on tomorrow, Deidre mused herself, before falling quickly into a lust-filled deep sleep.

Chapter 4
House of Confessions

Deidre woke up later than usual the next morning, still feeling somewhat euphoric from the unexpected and long night before. She decided to lounge lazily in her bed for a little while before getting her day started, something she rarely did. Deidre was unable to divert her thoughts from the previous night's surprising events, or from Carlo. He had really taken her pleasantly by surprise and piqued her interest. She had never met anyone quite like him before, and she dwelled on thoughts of him while turning on her bedroom television. Perhaps watching the morning news for a change she could divert her mind from thoughts of this fascinating new stranger.

But frenzied and fiery fantasies of Carlo doused any chance of her having any serious interest in what was on the TV. Instead, the frolicking flames prompted a need to temporarily extinguish Daria's own sexual flames. She knew she would have to quell her passions before she could focus on anything else.

Having wakened from her erotically captive daydreaming, and after a little playtime with her vibrator, she set off to the kitchen to make a pot of coffee and get started with her day. She knew she had a lot of catching up to do on household chores, as well as needing to make notes with reference to her busy upcoming work week before going to Gregory's. Checking on her very unstable schizophrenic patient Katrina was one of the reminders at the top of the list.

Upon arriving at Gregory's home at three o'clock, she let herself in and headed out to the patio, where she could see that Gregory had been working hard to set up the outside table for their weekly chat. Gregory has gone all out this time, she thought to herself as she noticed it was decorated elegantly with fine china and even cloth napkins, instead of the everyday dishes and paper napkins she was used to seeing.

There were some luscious looking hors d'oeuvres, as well as a beautiful flower arrangement, which Gregory had created out of assorted colorful flowers from his garden, even tucking in some roses, which she could smell as soon as she neared the table. Gregory is so talented, Deidre thought to herself, as she made her way to the charmingly set table.

"You've really outdone yourself this time, Gregory," Deidre said as she sat down, adding "The table setting looks absolutely beautiful, and the snacks look simply scrumptious! And I see that you pulled out the good china as well."

"Welcome, Deidre. It's good to see you again, dear. I'm glad that you like it," Gregory said with a warm smile and a kiss on her cheek. "So what in the world have you done now that I should know about?" He smirked as he spoke.

"Oh, Gregory, you're not going to believe this!" Deidre began, as she placed a napkin on her lap. Gregory immediately busied himself perusing the three bottles of wine Deidre had brought for their Sunday afternoon cocktail party a/k/a therapy session. She felt these weekly meetings to be important to both her sanity and her life.

"Ahhh...I think we'll start off with this interesting looking wine," Gregory said, curiosity tingeing his voice as he popped the cork on the bottle of Château la Confession.

Deidre enjoyed the opportunities that she had to socialize with Gregory. It was better than having a female friend at times like this, she thought to herself. She could divulge the most delicate and intimate of situations in full detail with Gregory without him becoming jealous, or judgmental of her.

"Oh my God, Gregory! There was the most gorgeous hunk at the club last night," Deidre started. "He was tall and lean, with golden light-brown hair that glistened, and... fucking unbelievable sex appeal." Her beaming grin, although worth a thousand words, was not nearly worthy of representation of the surreally erotic experience that she had had the night before. Deidre went on to explain the events on the dance floor that had led up to the darkened bathroom hallway seduction scene.

"He caught me totally by surprise and pulled me off into the shadows in the hallway. And before I could even think to respond, he grabbed my hair and pulled my head backward." She was unable to conceal, let alone even understand, her own sexual feelings and fascination for a stranger she had just met. And Deidre could see clearly that Gregory was now in a complete state of shock, captivated by her story so far.

"You've got to be kidding, Deidre!" Gregory sounded skeptical.

"I wouldn't joke about something like this, Gregory. There's no way I could make this stuff up!" She declared with further details added. "And without warning or permission, he began kissing me up and down my throat, neck, and chest, in a most come-hither manner. It was like something straight out of a torrid fantasy movie. I couldn't believe it! I was instantly intrigued and wanted him to do so much more." It was true confessions time, but as she recounted the story, Gregory wasn't the only one amazed. Deidre could hardly believe it herself.

"Holy shit!" Gregory exclaimed. "Weren't you the least bit afraid? How in the hell do you get yourself into these sorts of situations, Deidre?" Gregory was now leaning forward in his chair with furled eyebrows, a look of concern crossing his face. Refilling his wine glass, he said "Well, Deidre, I am sure you must have some interesting explanation, right?!" His tone was humorously sarcastic, in character for the man.

"I have no fucking clue how this happened, Gregory." Deidre's tone showed that she was as surprised and baffled as he was. She looked around the table, seeing that Gregory had made some of her favorite snacks for the occasion. There were small plates of sausage-stuffed mushrooms, shrimp cocktail, burrata, and olive tapenade crostini, all which she knew to be fairly time-consuming to prepare. He had even cut up some fresh seasonal fruits, to which Deidre helped herself, realizing that she had been so preoccupied with her thoughts during the day that she had not eaten much at all.

"I can't tell you exactly what it was, or why," Deidre said as she quickly inhaled several crostini and then reached for a piece of shrimp, "but there was something magical about that moment, Gregory. I could feel amazing and fiery passion in him."

"And, as aggressively as it may sound like he behaved—and he did….." Her voice trailed off for a few seconds while she relived the scene in her mind and then laughed. "Never once did I feel any reason for concern. I strangely felt no reason to be afraid, Gregory," she explained in amused astonishment. "In fact, it was absolutely heavenly…. I didn't want the moment to end. I had goosebumps over my entire body. That's the best way to explain it."

Gregory seemed to be momentarily at a loss for words. He put his fork down to give Deidre his full attention as she continued to recount every sordid detail of the previous night. She knew full well that what had occurred was completely out of the norm—or, at least, it was out of the norm in most people's daily lives. But in her world, strange occurrences seemed to be the norm.

"So, did you call this Carlo character today and make any dinner plans?" Gregory inquired, now rolling his eyes at her in disbelief and then letting out a heavy sigh.

"Of course I did," Deidre replied. "We're meeting downtown tonight at seven o'clock for dinner. He's taking me to Ruth's Chris steakhouse!" Her voice carried a hint of teasing snobbery. She was clearly pleased and impressed with Carlo's restaurant choice.

"Wow, nice! Why can't I meet someone like that?" Gregory responded.

After filling Gregory in on the rest of the events of the strange scene, Deidre claimed "This was a-once-in-a-lifetime occurrence,

Gregory," before falling silent with a broad smile. Then, with a dreamy stare, Deidre gazed out into Gregory's painstakingly well-groomed yard to see rose bushes in full bloom, off in the distance. Fully engulfed in a sexually charged moment of reflection, Deidre was at first unaware that Gregory had briefly left the table to turn on some music. Then she recognized the beginning of a hauntingly bittersweet tune, one that she had not heard in a while: "Sweet Child o' Mine," by Aerosmith. The melody immediately began to invade her psyche, tugging at its very core and threatening her good humor with its words, sound, and painful relevance to her life, as it always did.

Her thoughts were immediately catapulted back to a "true love," once again, whom she had known and lost. It was Neal, the same man whom she had been reminiscing about several nights earlier, when her answering service had thankfully called, interrupting her sadness. Why can't my damn service call now, and interrupt this loneliness I'm feeling without you, Neal! she thought to herself in sorrow, as unwelcome tears began to well in her eyes.

The song had been one of Neal's favorites, and he told Deidre years before that it always reminded him of her. Deidre glanced up briefly at the beautifully cloudless late afternoon sky, the view of which was blurred by the pools of tears she fought to hold back as she wondered to herself if he was looking down on her now, from afar. Deidre missed him so much. But more than anything else, she missed what could have been but never was, and now never could be.

Deidre found it increasingly hard to conceal her sadness as the song played on, and soon she felt a rogue tear escape down her cheek. She quickly pulled her napkin from her lap and wiped it away before Gregory could notice, and softly exclaimed "Dammit!" in subdued frustration. She really didn't want to talk about Neal right now, knowing she would completely break down weeping.

The two had met through Sean, a mutual friend of both, several years earlier. In fact, she did not particularly care for him very much when they initially met, finding him to be somewhat arrogant, bordering on being what she considered an asshole. But there was also an undeniably strange and strong chemistry between the two, nearly on sight. The chemistry was so strong, in fact, that by the end of that first night that they met, the two had gone from annoyance with one another to torrid lovemaking. It was something Deidre would never forget.

A shortage of beds in the resort hotel where Deidre and Sean were sharing a hotel room created an issue one evening. Neal had driven quite a distance to visit Sean, unexpectedly, and did not want to make the long drive home after drinking, but there were only two twin beds in the room. He had to choose between sleeping in a bed with Deidre or with their mutual friend, another male. And so now, with seeming sincerity, Neal promised Deidre that he would not touch her if she'd allow him to share her bed.

With decision-making skills impaired from the excessive partying earlier that evening, Deidre felt no pain or sense of restraint, so she reluctantly agreed, warning him to stay on his side of the small bed.

But within a very short period of time after they were tightly tucked in for the night to sleep—or so she thought—Deidre could hear and feel Neal's body heat and rate of breathing increase, and she could smell him now. Clearly uncomfortable, Neal continued shifting himself on the bed to switch positions, while being careful not to touch her. Why can't he just be still! Deidre wondered in silence. But very quickly, Deidre began to realize the answer to her own question, keenly sensing without a shadow of a doubt that Neal was feeling the same explosive temptation she was. And Deidre's very accurate perception would became confirmed as Neal's hand began to slowly wander over to gently caress her inviting backside as she lay facing away from him. One thing quickly escalated to another, as she succumbed to his uninvited yet desired and welcomed invasion of her. And then it was "game on!" she remembered.

At nearly six-foot four, and with very broad shoulders, Neal scooped Deidre up in his strong arms with ease and carried her into the relative privacy of the bathroom. As he held her body tightly with one arm, he quickly and efficiently cleared the counter's contents off to one side in one fell swoop with his free arm, and then sat her gently down on the now-clear countertop. It had been an unbelievable and incredible moment of intense passion, Deidre now silently remembered to herself. She would never forget how amazing and wildly free Neal had made love to her that night in the bathroom, as their mutual friend Sean, just outside the door, in the bedroom, struggled to sleep despite the noise.

Their fiery and tumultuous love affair would last for a year, until Deidre could no longer deny her love for him, wanting more with him than just an affair. She wanted a real relationship, something he could not give her at the time. Deidre was forced to accept reality, and that reality included the fact that he would never leave the dysfunctional long-term relationship he was in with another woman.

Knowing herself to have fallen in love with someone who would not be available anytime soon if ever, Deidre painfully called off the affair, telling him that life was too short to waste, waiting for someone she could never have. She knew in her heart that she would not and could not settle any longer for anything less than being someone's "one and only." Deidre would repeat that same phrase on more than one occasion in conversation with Neal, as well as with several others over the years to come—regretfully, always with men she had begun to fall in love with.

Neal did not take the news very well and became angry with Deidre for not wanting to see him again. But Deidre knew in her heart and soul that it would not work out between them, at least not until he was available, if he ever would be. Deidre spent a number of days and lonely nights agonizing over the decision she had made, crying for the man she knew she could not have.

Some time after breaking off her affair and losing contact with Neal, Deidre learned from their mutual friend that he had developed a terminal illness. Feeling completely distraught, Deidre wanted so badly to reach out to him, to tell him that she loved him, but she figured that to be a bad idea, as neither he nor his family needed any additional or unnecessary complications or stress at such a delicate time. The news of Neal's death shortly afterward hit Deidre hard, leaving her to feel helpless, and then devoid of emotion for some time. Deidre knew that Neal must have replayed her words to him over and over again.

Both Deidre and Gregory had remained silent as the song played, but now it came to a finish, with Deidre's thoughts still floundering in a hazy fog of depressed reminiscence. Finally Gregory broke the silence, saying, "You'll have to call me tomorrow, Deidre, and let me know how dinner goes with Carlo tonight. I wish I could be a fly on the wall."

"For sure!" Deidre replied, feeling grateful for having Gregory as a friend to talk to, and grateful too that he had inadvertently distracted and redirected her thoughts from Neal, back to a pleasant topic. Deidre then realized that she had not told him her funny and somewhat embarrassing story from that morning. It was a tale she knew she could share with no one other than Gregory, and she knew that he would love it.

"But there's something else I'm going to tell you now, Gregory, and you're really going to laugh your ass off!" Deidre said. She then told Gregory that early in the morning, she had wakened feeling horny, after being fired up by the unexpected and captivating interaction with Carlo the night before. And that she then decided to take matters into her own hands literally as well as figuratively, and she masturbated with one of her favorite vibrators.

"Why am I not surprised, Deidre?" Gregory was unable to

contain his laughter at how freely Deidre spoke of such personal things.

"Dammit, Gregory! Can you just be quiet and listen for a minute?!" Deidre chided with a laugh. "I haven't even gotten to the good part yet!"

"Well, you orgasmed, didn't you?" Gregory was toying with her in return.

"Of course I did, silly. But it's what happened next that you're going to love." Deidre then went on to explain that, once she reached a most awesome climax, she put her toy away in the nightstand, feeling amazingly relaxed. Knowing she had an hour to spare, she decided to take a quick nap to refuel after the previous long night and to be ready for that night's possible activities. So now, with her pink friend back in its special stowage space, she fell back onto the bed, satiated for the time being.

But just when she was about to drift off into a very pleasant sleep state, she could hear an annoying sound interfering with her tranquility. A rapid pounding sound invaded Deidre's much-needed repose, creating a very unwelcome and unwanted disturbance.

She lay in her bed, patiently awaiting the non-stop bothersome battering to stop, and recalling that the next door neighbors had been pressure-cleaning their driveway and the walkways surrounding their home the day before. She thought, however, that the work had been completed.

After what she considered to be a more-than-reasonable amount of time had passed, she decided she could stand it no longer. Thoroughly agitated now, Deidre left the comfort of her bed in search of the unpleasant distraction. But as she got up to peer out the window, she quickly became aware that the repetitive pounding sound was actually coming from a much closer location.

As she told this to Gregory, she began to giggle, and soon he as well as she broke into hysterical laughter as he realized what must have happened. She confirmed it. "Yes, Gregory! My fucking vibrator had rolled in the drawer after I closed it, and somehow it had turned itself on! I kid you not, Gregory, the motherfucker was vibrating away in the drawer for probably ten minutes. Can you only imagine?!" Neither she nor Gregory was able to compose himself or herself from their hysterical laughter for at least a few minutes afterward.

"It's a damn good thing I keep spare batteries!" Deidre quipped as they both finally stopped laughing and caught their breath.

Gregory reached for the wine bottle to replenish their libations, only to realize the bottle was empty.

"Okay, Deidre," Gregory said. "So, which wine should we polish off next? The Ménage à Trois, the Ball-Buster, or the new blend I found? What are we going to talk about next, so I can serve the correct wine? And by the way, the Château was absolutely delicious. I love the lingering hint of licorice. It would be perfect with some beef bourguignon."

"No, dear," Deidre said, smiling. "There are no more tales for the day. And you are so right about the wine, Gregory. "But it sure as hell wasn't cheap. It was almost $60 for the bottle. But I know how much you cherish your Cab-Sav blends. And seriously, with that name? House of confession? How à propos, especially for our rendezvous today! Don't you agree?"

"I couldn't agree with you more, Deidre," Gregory replied, relaxing back into his chair once again.

"Oh yes—there is one other thing," Deidre said. "I received a text this morning from Roger. You remember Roger, my raucous rock 'n' roller, whom I haven't seen in months!" Excitement tinged her voice.

"I swear, Deidre, you are never at a loss for a man, are you?" As he spoke, Gregory poured more wine into each of their glasses.

"Not as long as there's life left in this body, baby!" Deidre responded. "I just keep checking more things off my bucket list.

You know how I feel, Gregory. You only live once! And hopefully, one day I will finally meet, and be able to settle down with, just one man." She gazed off into the distance, in more somber thought once again.

Deidre did enjoy her savage sex life, but she sincerely desired, more than anything, to settle down with just one man. She hated going home to an empty house each evening, and loathed the emptiness she felt inside herself when she slept and awoke alone.

"So, Deidre, when will you be seeing Roger again?" Gregory queried.

"Not sure yet," Deidre answered. "He said that the band would be playing a gig nearby soon, and that he would get me further info once he had a confirmed schedule. I have so much fun with him! He's not just handsome and amazing in bed—he's also incredibly smart, and funny too!"

"Well then, you'll have to keep me abreast of the details. And speaking of breasts," Gregory said, "your breasts look fantastic in that dress, Deidre!"

"Thanks, cutie. You're always so sweet. I guess I should wear this one more often. You don't think it's a little too slutty?" Deidre asked.

"Not at all, Deidre! You look hot!" Gregory replied, a mischievous smile crossing his face.

Deidre knew that Gregory had had a crush on her for years. But she made it a practice to refrain from taking relationships with those she worked with beyond anything more than just friendship, no matter how attracted she might have been to them. She didn't want relationship ups and downs to interfere with her work. And besides, she felt Gregory to be an invaluable friend, and she did not want to lose that. Whenever Gregory would become overly flirtatious with her, Deidre would lightheartedly reply, "You know, Gregory, lovers fall by the wayside left and right, but friends are forever," to which Gregory would always reply disappointedly, "I know."

It was now nearing five-thirty in the evening, and Deidre knew that she needed to get home to freshen up before her dinner date with Carlo, which was scheduled for just an hour and a half from then. She told Gregory that it was time for her to be heading out, and that he should keep the other bottles of wine she had brought, to use in next week's therapy session. Then the two of them got up from the table and began carrying the leftover food and dishes into the kitchen.

But while the two were busy clearing the table and putting everything back in place, Deidre could sense from Gregory's newly subdued manner, coupled with an uneasy silence, that he was unhappy both with her impending departure and with the fact that she was meeting another man for dinner.

Once the clean-up was complete, Gregory told Deidre hesitantly, with affection, that he wished she could have stayed longer, but Deidre knew it was time to go. And so after hugging Gregory and giving him a quick kiss on the cheek, she said, "Goodbye, mi amore, until tomorrow. I'll see you back at the office. And in the meantime, Gregory dear, don't do anything I wouldn't do!"

Gregory let out a hearty laugh at that, and then said, "Oh, right! I should be saying that to you, Deidre! Have a good time tonight, and I'll expect a full report in the morning."

Deidre laughed as she left Gregory's home, en route for her own to get ready to meet up with Carlo for dinner and, hopefully, for an exotic dessert, with a carnal and kinky flavor. This will be quite an interesting evening, she thought with wonderment, as erotic fantasies played out in her mind, successfully occupying and entertaining her thoughts during her drive home.

Chapter 5
Dinner and Dessert, with a Side of Didactic Direction

God only knows what will happen tonight! Deidre thought poignantly as she prepared herself to be the steamy main course at dinner tonight with Carlo. After carefully touching up her make-up in the bathroom mirror, Deidre chose some of her most provocative clothes from the closet. Her intentions and sights were set on blowing the gorgeous stranger away. She felt certain she could land him, hook, line, and sinker, as she removed a beautifully embellished black dress and a pair of spiked heels from her sexy wardrobe. She decided on wearing a lacy black push-up bra with matching black thong panties to finish the effect. Just in case, she thought to herself humorously, as she felt certain it would be more like preparing for when the inevitable would occur.

After spritzing on some of her favorite perfume, Deidre further dabbed the carefully chosen scent in just the right places before setting out for the thirty-minute drive to the steakhouse to meet Carlo. She arrived to see him perched casually on a barstool, chatting and laughing with the bartender. She immediately thought him to be even more sexually appealing tonight than he had been the previous night.

The first thing Deidre noticed was his well-tailored white linen button-down shirt, unbuttoned perfectly at the top, so that she could see his golden skin aglow, accentuating his gorgeous smile. A dark blue sport coat with brown suede elbow patches hung well over his muscled shoulders. A classy accessory to the tightly fitted blue jeans, Deidre thought, as she panned farther to see an exotic pair of European boots. Interesting, she thought, curiously pleased with his wardrobe choices.

He is smoking hot! Deidre thought as she sauntered over to where Carlo was seated, with Carlo glancing over and smiling as he watched her approaching.

Deidre could feel Carlo's eyes examining her as she watched him during those intense few moments of analysis. She could sense an instant smoldering heat between the two of them and could not wait to investigate its source of ignition even further. Their eyes remained completely locked on one another, with their combined energies and hormones, creating a powerfully sensual vortex.

Carlo rose from his seat as Deidre neared, pulling out the chair next to him for her to sit in, and then pushing it in once she was seated. What a gentleman. A sweet smelling, hot as fuck gentleman. Like he walked straight out of GQ kind of hot! she surmised, as he leaned in and nuzzled her cheek teasingly with his nose, saying "It's nice to see you again, beautiful." Deidre's keen sense of smell recognized his very heady cologne as he softly kissed her on the cheek. She struggled to remain composed as her senses became excited by his unusually erotic aroma as well as his sensual beauty.

The two ordered drinks, engaging in small talk for a few minutes, until their table became ready. Little did Deidre know that Carlo had requested a specially located table, with a bird's-eye view of the restaurant, yet secluded from the view of curious others nearby. A perfectly romantic location, she thought when they were seated.

Deidre could sense Carlo's desire for her, his wanting to devour her, and it excited her. It was unlike anything she had ever experienced until that moment, and it was powerfully provocative. As their conversation progressed from small talk to topics more in depth and deeply personal in nature, she could see the fire in his eyes growing even stronger.

The duo would enjoy a magically luscious dinner of filet mignon and lobster by candlelight, paired with a perfect red wine and undeniable, internal sizzling embers. Deidre found herself unable to resist Carlo's powerful force and message. She knew without a shadow of a doubt that she and Carlo, would be spending some time together tonight. And it would turn out to be a night that would prove excitingly sexual in nature among other things—some pleasurable, some not.

Nearing the end of dinner, Deidre found herself completely distracted with fantasies of making wild love with Carlo. She wanted to feel him wrap his arms, legs, and entire being around hers. The desire to feel him inside her overwhelmed her every thought, making it difficult for her to focus on conversation. She wanted him to fuck her right then and there.

Actually signing on for more than she realized at that moment, Deidre was feeling profoundly taken in by his nearly golden light brown eyes, boring a hole through her. The energy behind his virile focus rendered her instantly powerless and defenseless against him.

As Carlo and Deidre finally finished their dinner and discussed plans for the evening, it became evident that Carlo, too, had plans for the evening. And coming to Deidre's was at the very top of the plan he had.

Consumed now by Carlo's charm as well as his powerfully protective and sensual nature Deidre succumbed in a moment of weakness, blinded by her own animalistic desire, thus allowing herself to be vulnerable at a time and with a man, she should not have ever been weakened by, or with. Unaware of the imminent consequences at that moment, Deidre indulged herself in a false sense of security with the wrong man.

"Would you care for some dessert?" the waiter asked, breaking into the steamy dream state Deidre had been mentally lost in. Deidre was impressed to learn that Carlo had thought to reserve such a perfectly located spot. She admired the beautiful view around her, but especially the view of the gorgeous male specimen next to her. She looked over to see the waiter patiently awaiting an answer, having no awareness of the most exciting, primal pondering he had just interrupted. Deidre felt annoyed by the intrusion at such a sensually exciting and rare moment.

"Why don't we get dessert to go, Deidre?" Carlo asked, while perusing the dessert menu with obvious disinterest.

"That sounds like a great idea," Deidre replied, as she imagined the real dessert that she intended on sharing with Carlo later. As she spoke, she became aware of a hand working its way up her thigh.

"Why don't you pick, my dear," Carlo said, handing the dessert menu over to Deidre with his free hand, surely having no idea of how far into the night her fantasies had already begun to travel. But the fantasies grew in their intensity as Carlo's fingers inched their way up her dress. Thank God the tablecloth is long, Deidre thought.

"Do you like crème brûlée, Carlo?" Deidre asked, looking into Carlo's eyes, which were eagerly watching her for a response and seemed ready to be rid of the waiter, as well.

"I love crème brûlée!" Carlo replied, donning a devilish grin, observing Deidre's expression and reaction as his fingers ventured farther up her dress.

You don't give a fuck what we order for dessert. Deidre acknowledged Carlo in a mutual meeting of the eyes, smiles, and minds, with no further words necessary. The chemistry between Deidre and Carlo during those moments was fantastically torturing.

"So crème brûlée it is! Please make one up to go, and we will take our check as well," he instructed the waiter with a voice and mannerisms commanding dismissal, then turning his full attention back to Deidre's waiting desire and delirium.

"I would like to stop by your place for just a little while to learn more about you, Deidre, if it's okay with you? And to have dessert as well, of course," Carlo concluded, leaning back into his chair now, in a relaxed position, with his hands resting on his well-muscled thighs. From where Deidre sat, she could see that Carlo felt in charge of both this moment and the upcoming night's events. She could also see that his cock was rock hard

64

beneath his tight jeans, and realized she herself was becoming wetter by the minute.

Leaning forward and taking Deidre's hands in his, Carlo stared into her already-dreaming eyes. The way that Carlo's glistening hair surrounded his handsomely strong chiseled face reminded Deidre of a stunning lion. And in the erotically exotic sense, she knew she was a lioness in heat tonight, and she had just met her lion. Her needs for prowling for this night would clearly be filled.

You are not just coming over to get to know me, and for dessert, she recognized in Carlo's animalistic stare. You're coming over to get to know me and then having me for dessert, Deidre swiftly surmised, with a returned expression and demeanor, telling of planned agreement and compliance. Seeing instantly that the fire in Carlo's eyes was by comparison more intense, she began to sense a twinge of ownership coming over her and felt confused as to whether it was good or bad. It certainly made her a bit uncomfortable at that moment of perplexing passion. Sex tonight, though, would not be deferred by anything, Deidre knew. There was a fire between her and Carlo that needed to be addressed.

Carlo followed Deidre home that night. She didn't worry too much about his returning unannounced, as she lived in a gated community.

Upon entering the house, Deidre showed Carlo around and offered him a drink. She lit some candles and turned on sultry music before going to the kitchen to make their drinks. As Deidre stood at the counter mixing drinks, she could feel a hand sliding up each side of her short dress, in an attempt to free her of her clothing. With a venereal sigh, Deidre set the glass in her hand back on the counter, relaxing and succumbing to the moment and subsequent movements.

Deidre turned to face Carlo just as he was pulling her dress over her head. He dropped it to the floor with an admiring smile as Deidre stood wantonly gazing at him in her black, lacy thong panties and bra.

"Let me help you with that, sexy," Carlo said, reaching around Deidre's back and releasing her bra clasp, allowing her breasts to bounce out freely, escaping their captivity. She hated wearing a bra.

"Much better," Carlo said with a pleased sigh at the sight of Deidre's bare breasts. Her nipples were erect, more from anticipation than from the cool night air.

Immediately reached out and cupping Deidre's breasts with his hands, Carlo began kissing her deeply, forcing her backward against the counter. Deidre then reached up and wrapped her arms around Carlo's neck, pulling him in closer to her, sensing a constrained, rigid presence in his pants, eagerly awaiting its own escape.

Taking Carlo's hand in hers, Deidre led him to the couch, strategically positioning herself so that she could sit down and unbutton his jeans as he stood in front of her. His expression showed that he was enjoying each and every minute.

As Carlo stood in front of Deidre, with his pants pulled down to his thighs now, she could see the outline and outpouching of Carlo's arousal, and removed it from its very restrictive hiding place. With inviting delight, Carlo's cock made its way to her mouth, exactly where she wanted it to be.

"Mmmm," Deidre moaned with pleasure as she sucked him and tasted his sweet pre-cum, feeling his strong hands on her shoulders as he brace himself while his hips pumped his cock in and out of her mouth.

"Fuck, fuck, fuck!" he cried out, as Deidre took him all the way down her throat, posed now on her knees in front of him, taking charge of the moment. She so loved these times, she thought, peering up to see Carlo's expression as he struggled to remain composed.

"I want to come inside you," Carlo said intently as he pulled Deidre to a standing position from the couch and began kissing her passionately. She could feel his body becoming damp with sweat, and loved his smell.

Carlo began kissing Deidre's thighs, teasing her with his tongue in all the right places. Deidre's body responded to his actions. She was determined and ready to take this night's pleasure to the next level. And once Carlo began to suck on Deidre's breasts, there would be no applicable speed limit placed on the night's action.

Making their way to the bedroom, Carlo hastily pulled Deidre's panties off with a fierceness that bordered on aggression. Standing naked in front of her now, Carlo eased Deidre back onto the bed and mounted her with audible pleasure.

Deidre reached up over her head to grasp her pillow, in a weak attempt to hold on as Carlo rammed himself into her. As forceful as he was with her, she did not want it to stop, and her actions would convey her message of desired continuance.

"Yes, keep going, baby," Deidre exclaimed. "I'm going to come."

"Then we will come together," Carlo seethed as he staved off his own orgasm, to meet the timing of hers.

Deidre writhed with pleasure as she came wildly, with Carlo's throbbing cock buried deep inside her now. Carlo's breathing became heavier as he released himself into her in frozen fury.

"Wow! That was fucking amazing!" Carlo exclaimed as they both made their way up to the top of the bed and collapsed in sweaty exhaustion.

"Yes, it was," she agree.

As the two lay resting, Deidre began to wonder if Carlo intended staying for the night, or if he planned on making the hour-long drive home. While she had just been sexually satiated, she was not entirely comfortable going to sleep with her handsome new lover.

"Will you be all right to drive home tonight?" Deidre asked apprehensively. "I know it's a long way. Maybe I should make you some coffee before you leave."

A little puzzled, Carlo said, "I would like to stay over tonight, but the drive shouldn't be bad this time of night."

Deidre felt somewhat uneasy and annoyed with how comfortable Carlo was already making himself in her home and her bed. He was moving too quickly for her liking, and she wanted a good night's sleep, by herself.

"I'm going to clean up," Deidre said as she headed to the bathroom to shower, with Carlo soon following suit.

"When can I see you again?" Carlo asked, pinning Deidre against the shower wall, with his hands on either side of her.

"Maybe next weekend?" Deidre replied as she playfully slipped out of Carlo's reach, quickly drying off and putting on a nightie, to stop Carlo from staring at her "in that way," afraid things would become heated again.

"I was thinking of tomorrow night, if you are available," he said, watching Deidre for a response.

"No can do, I already have plans. I have an old friend stopping by for drinks after work tomorrow," she replied. It's definitely not an old friend, Deidre thought to herself. In fact, it's a new and very young friend!

"Okay then, will you give me a call tomorrow, so we can set something up?" Carlo asked with a display of impatience.

"I will, I will," Deidre replied as she began walking toward the front door to expedite Carlo's exit.

"Then I will speak with you in the morning, beautiful," Carlo affirmed before giving her a passionate kiss and leaving.

"Whew!" Deidre sighed aloud. I didn't think I'd ever get him out of here! Relieved, she headed for her waiting bed. There is something about him I just don't care for, she reflected. But she just couldn't put her finger on exactly what it was that bothered her about him. For tonight, however, Deidre put her concerns and thoughts on hold and fell fast asleep.

This strange sixth sense, which Deidre had always had but had only recently learned to listen to, sent up a yellow flag. It meant that Deidre needed to put up a cautionary shield, at least for a while. And so she did, but not until the lion and his lioness had met and mated wildly on a few occasions, each of which left Deidre to feel as though Carlo had dug his claws into her deeper after each visit. And there was no way that Deidre could allow such savage ownership of her soul, she knew.

Sex with Carlo was always wildly uninhibited, never boring. Their intense sessions would travel throughout various rooms, until they most usually finished in the bedroom, and then collapsed in exhaustion.

She loved the way he dominated her sexually, aggressively removing her panties as he bent her over the living room couch on short notice. But Carlo's sexual attributes were overshadowed by a dark side, which was coming to light. Carlo was quickly making himself too comfortable in Deidre's home and her life. He snooped through her things and posed himself arrogantly, while he simultaneously posed and positioned himself in her world. The dominance he intended over Deidre could even be felt in his voice messages and texts, which she felt bordered obsession. And Deidre began to realize quickly that she was potentially getting into real trouble with Carlo.

The rapidly escalating degree of claustrophobia she began to feel outweighed some of the most amazing and free sex that Deidre would ever experience. But seriously, Deidre, it's time to go! her primal survival tactic would scold, as it came to life to watch over her in full force, and instructing her as to how she needed to handle the situation. This was something that Deidre found hard to explain to most. Her inner core, being, and soul relied on those unexplainable senses, which had protected her from so much for most of her life.

Deidre never sought to capitalize on her life's decisions in the dollar sense, only in that she would not settle for, nor would she be content with, anything less than the best when it came to her heart and soul, the core of her being.

Yet, in spite of the intense desire that Deidre was feeling for Carlo now, her deepest core was telling her to be careful of this man whom she had first met "in the shadows." She was being warned that there were more shadows and dark places to come, and thankfully she listened. She would unleash her loosely knit plan to extricate Carlo from her life with no hard feelings. Deidre's foresight would prove to be successful proactively, when combined with her accurately aimed damage control instincts, and "slam dunk," it would work. Deidre's soul was deeper than any of her suitors could have ever imagined, so when her cautionary flags were erected, she listened and created a foolproof plan to suit whatever the situation required.

Deidre strategically planned to exhaust Carlo's interest in her by making herself inaccessible for various reasons and it worked, satisfying her most humanistic point of view-driven plan in life, to never bring harm unnecessarily to anyone.

And as Deidre was putting her plans in motion with Carlo, she received a message from Jerry, asking, "What's up?"

Deidre knew that she couldn't lead Jerry on any longer and dialed Jerry's number one last time, in order to cut those unaffordable ties as well before the noose became much tighter. Jerry became furious with Deidre's saying that she could not see him anymore. She continued to reiterate to Jerry that, "If I allow this to continue any longer, I would only be leading you on."

After which, Jerry let out a litany of expletives and angrily ordered her to lose his number before hanging up on her.

"Wow!" Deidre said out loud, in bittersweet relief that that was now behind her, and knowing she would not hear from Jerry anymore. But the memories of the wild and crazy nights they had spent together would always bring a smile to her face, especially when she needed to adjust her headboard for some mundane reason.

Monday morning arrived, as it always did, and Deidre knew that her workload was going to increase this week, hopefully keeping her out of any further trouble. But that was just a fleeting delusion. Her life was normally abnormal.

Deidre spoke with Katrina's mom early in the day, finding Katrina and her infant to be well and staying with her and her husband. Deidre rescheduled Katrina's appointment, impressing on the mom the importance of Katrina's attendance at her upcoming appointments, as well as the need for her to be regimentally responsible with her medications and diet. Deidre concluded the conversation by saying, "Call me if there are any changes, or if you have any serious concerns," before hanging up. Katrina's mom had become very adept in dealing with her daughter's lifelong mental illness. And Dr. Deidre Villanova knew that if Katrina's mom did call, it was something that needed attention.

At least the crisis has been averted for the moment, Deidre thought to herself. Yet Deidre was unable to shake the unsettled gut feeling of her instinct telling her not to rest on her laurels, or trouble with Katrina would soon return. Staying in touch with Katrina would prove to be advantageous, allowing Deidre to intervene at the early onset of problems, lessening the drama.

The growing laundry list of patients whom Deidre would treat during the week turned into a blur, with no one seeming out of the ordinary—that is, no one except Mr. Lawrence Leary. And even his complaints and issues were ordinary. But Mr. Leary's son, Thomas, was another story. There was something very unusual about him, Deidre noticed the moment they met, when Thomas brought his aging father to Dr. Deidre Villanova for help. He had been struggling with depression since losing his wife.

It was clear to Deidre right away that Mr. Leary and his late wife, Sophia, had experienced a wonderful life together, raising two children in a small community that nurtured a family way of life, instead of in the big city. And further devastating was the fact that they had been together since high school. Deidre knew that it was not uncommon in these situations for the surviving spouse to pass away as well, fairly soon after losing his or her love. Wishing to stave off an unnecessarily hastened second death in the Leary family, Deidre spent additional time discussing the impending risks and circumstances with Mr. Leary's son, Thomas.

As Deidre spent time with Thomas, the undeniable nuances became stronger and began to leave Dr. Villanova confused as to how she should deal with him and her patient, feeling as though she might be muddying her own ethical rules. She did not approve of becoming romantically involved with her patients' family members while the patients were still in therapy.

Dr. Villanova continued treating Mr. Leary, and coaching his son after each visit on bereavement support groups and various socialization activities, which she felt Mr. Leary could benefit from, continuing to disregard the nuances she felt Thomas to be conveying. But after four weeks of her seeing Mr. Leary and his son, Thomas finally broke the ice at the conclusion of one of their meetings. He asked Deidre to dinner, stating that he found her to be "fascinating and beautiful."

"For seafood, Chinese, or even just a drink, to talk informally," he said. "I promise to be a perfect gentleman and return you unharmed." As he spoke, his face wore an intriguing smile.

"So, I take it you aren't married?" Deidre asked in as lighthearted a voice as she could command. It was a question that needed to be asked right up front, Deidre knew, as it seemed as though everyone had hidden baggage, which complicated the simplest of relationships.

"It's complicated," Thomas replied, adding, "We haven't slept together in years, but that's another story, which we can discuss over dinner, maybe this weekend? May I call you Deidre, Dr. Villanova?"

Deidre felt a wave of uncertainty about getting involved with a man who was still in any type of relationship, but she sensed a level of sincerity in him and was attracted to his kind and gentle spirit.

"Okay, Thomas," she said apprehensively, standing in front of him with her arms crossed in front of her, protecting her personal space for the moment. "How about I touch base with you on Thursday, when I have a better idea of my schedule for the week's end, and the weekend?" She favored him with a curious smile.

"Excellent!" Thomas replied, removing a business card from his wallet and scribbling his private cell number on it before giving it to Deidre. "I'll be waiting to hear from you, Deidre." Then he turned to leave her office.

What the fuck am I doing? Deidre asked herself as she sat back down at her desk and leaned back in her chair in deep thought, before making notes on Mr. Leary's progress:

Mr. Leary remains somewhat apathetic during therapy sessions, making little to no eye contact. He appears disinterested in outside support groups and shows little affect. I will continue to stress the importance of supplemental support to the family, in suggesting to the family that Mr. Leary may need to be placed on an anti-depressant. The patient's family remains actively involved in his care, Dr. Villanova noted before closing her patient file out for the day and seeing her next patient.

Thursday afternoon finally arrived, and Dr. Villanova could see that her schedule the next day would not be too heavy, so she decided to call Thomas to set up a tentative dinner meeting.

"Hello, this is Thomas Leary," she heard.

"Hey Thomas, it's Dr. Villanova—I mean Deidre," she said with a light chuckle.

"Well, hello there!" he exclaimed excitedly. "I didn't know if you'd really call."

"Well, I figured I'd give it a try, Thomas. Are you free tomorrow night, by chance?"

"I am after seven-thirty. Will that work for you?" he asked.

"Sure, Thomas," Deidre replied. "Where would you like to

meet?"

"Why don't we make this interesting and informal?" Thomas offered. "Would you be up for a sunset date at the beach? I find sunsets on the beach to be romantic. And then we can see where the night leads us from there."

Thomas and Deidre agreed on a well-known area of the beach as the spot to meet and then said their goodbyes before hanging up.

Early Friday afternoon, Deidre realized her schedule would be cleared earlier than usual, and she offered to drop her elderly neighbor's dog off at the veterinarian for boarding, as her neighbor was trying to get out of town to tend to a family emergency.

Deidre left her office for her home, wanting to change into a tank top and cut-off jean shorts. She expected her clothes to become fur-covered by the time she finished transporting the pet. Once she had dropped the precious pooch at the veterinarian's, Deidre stopped off at a convenience store for an iced tea. She felt like a scrounge as she stood next to her car, looking down to see her black tank top now covered in white dog hair.

After brushing off a respectable amount of the white fur from her clothes, Deidre went into the store and bought a drink, then returned to her car.

"Excuse me, miss?" Deidre heard as she was opening the driver side door in the nearing sunset sky. Quickly turning to face the voice, Deidre laid her eyes upon an absolutely gorgeous and very young man.

"Yes?" Deidre replied curiously, figuring he wanted to inquire about her muscle car, or maybe she had dropped something as she came out of the store.

With a radiant smile and curly brown locks, the very handsome young man asked, "Are you single?"

Standing next to her open car door now, Deidre answered "Yes, why?"

"Do you date younger men?" the curious cutie asked,

watching and waiting for Deidre's reply.

"I do now," Deidre answered, somewhat surprised by her own lack of hesitancy or caution. But the young man's sincerity and curiosity piqued Deidre's interest. She could see that he was rather naïve and shy, blushing as he approached her. You are very observant and perceptive, my friend, Deidre thought. You couldn't have chosen a more willing mentor—and certainly not a more eager one.

Deidre gave her new friend, Nate, her phone number, which he immediately stored into the contacts on his phone with a broad grin.

"Can I call you in an hour?" a very nubile Nate inquired.

"Sure! It was nice meeting you, Nate." Holy shit! Deidre screamed in her head. He's so fucking young! she jokingly scolded herself, but unsuccessfully. Deidre was unable to wipe the mischievous grin from her face for the entire twenty-minute drive home.

And as if on cue, Nate called Deidre just one hour later.

"So, when can I see you, and when can we hang out?" he asked with an eager voice.

"How about you come to my place tomorrow night, and we can talk and hang out by my pool?" Deidre asked. It would certainly not be cool for Dr. Deidre Villanova to be seen out in public with this very green young lover, a/k/a. protégé.

After receiving a call from Thomas postponing their sunset rendezvous, Deidre lay low that Friday night. In spite of feeling somewhat disappointed—although not entirely surprised—on hearing that Thomas had family affairs to deal with that evening, Deidre felt no need to venture out. She was actually feeling quite tranquil with her introspective happiness and knew that Nate would be coming over the next night, and he would scratch her itch. In return, she would teach him, satisfying him in a manner that only a more experienced woman could.

Deidre could only imagine Gregory's response this Sunday,

when she shared this tale at their weekly get-together.

Saturday went by uneventfully until about 4 o'clock, when Nate arrived, causing Deidre to become a lioness once again— but this time for a different reason. Nate was young and innocent, and when they'd met, she'd felt he didn't have a mean bone in his body.

In the brief period of time that the two had spent talking outside at the store, Deidre had been able to tell so much about Nate, starting the very moment he approached her. Nate told Deidre that he was a sports coach and came from a large family, which she realized must have been rather well heeled, with manners and presentation to back it up.

Nate arrived at Deidre's home with a nervous smile. She could sense that he was sweating bullets. Deidre knew that she had had some very good mentors and tutors. Feeling a powerful connection to this very young man, she set out to not only teach him but to satisfy him as well. Deidre also knew that this liaison would not continue. But she would enjoy the time while it lasted.

Preparing refreshments for the two while Nate went into the bathroom to put his bathing suit on, Deidre reflected on what a gorgeous afternoon it had been and felt relaxed after having indulged herself in the late-day fall sun prior to Nate's arrival. What a great way to end the day! her inner-soul screamed.

"The water is absolutely perfect!" Deidre told him, admiring the twenty-something-year-old tight body that now stood before her in his swim trunks.

Nate's eyes probed her, awaiting further instructions from his new "Mrs. Robinson," a/k/a Deidre. And she knew that tonight she would truly be a teacher, to her newest and so-very-handsome and eager pupil, who stood perfectly erect in front of her.

My, oh my, Deidre thought as Nate approached her, taking his drink from her. Without wasting much time, Deidre grabbed some towels and said, "Let's get wet," lightening the air in the room, and causing both to laugh as they headed out to Deidre's beautiful backyard pool, which was aglow with the most amazing iridescent blue lights, creating a perfect backdrop for the tiki torches she had already lighted. Her surround-sound stereo system piped music to further fill the air, already heavy with pheromones.

Without any words necessary, the two stepped into the pool, with Deidre walking to the deep end and stopping before the water reached her face. Upon turning back, she saw Nate coming toward her with a devilish yet nervous expression on his face. Once Nate reached Deidre, he immediately grabbed her, pulling her body into his. In response, Deidre's feet left the pool floor as she wrapped both her legs around his waist and her arms around his neck.

Deidre felt his erection beneath her, through the material of both her bathing suit and his swim trunks. Oh yeah, this will be quite enjoyable! Deidre's imagination alerted, as Nate carried them both over to the pool's edge. With obvious awkward movements showing his lack of experience, Nate untied Deidre's baiting suit top and tossed it on the deck, and then stood sensually admiring the way her breasts floated on the water's surface.

Deidre noticed at that moment how beautifully the flames from the tiki torches danced wildly across the surface of the water as if the water itself were on fire—and in more ways than one, it certainly was. Desiring Nate's very rigid and large penis, which kept poking at her through his trunks, she helped him to remove them, after which she removed her own bikini bottom.

As Norah Jones crooned sultry music in the background and flames danced around on the water's surface, Deidre and Nate turned the heat up even higher. Unable to resist each other any longer, Nate pulled Deidre into him again, with Deidre wrapping her legs around Nate's waist at just the perfect height to allow him to enter her all the way.

Now in a state of sheer ecstasy, Deidre felt shivers coursing through her entire body with the cooling night air, further helping to bring her nipples to their own full erection.

Both Nate and Deidre grew silent, with only the sounds of music and the water's movement to be heard, as they became entangled with one another. She could tell that he would come quickly, and she wanted to be ready for it and to enjoy it. She also wanted to make his orgasm memorable. Deidre wanted to be sure that this experience would surpass whatever fantasy Nate was wishing to fulfill with her.

Deidre took her young student to the shallow end of the pool, saying, "Let's try something different." She then turned to face into the side of the pool wall as Nate, not needing any further cue, entered her from behind, holding onto her shoulders, making pleased groaning sounds in her ear.

This is fucking amazing, Deidre thought to herself as she realized her orgasm nearing, and timing it perfectly to meet his.

"Oh my god that was awesome!" Nate exclaimed as Deidre turned to face him, giving him a long passionate kiss and then saying, "Yes, it was," but with only a partially satisfied smile. For Deidre knew that there would be more to come—in both senses of the word—before that night was over.

Telling Nate to stay where he was, Deidre stepped out of the pool to retrieve their drinks. Time slipped by quickly as the two lounged naked in the pool and talked, with Deidre finding herself impressed with her young lover's high level of maturity for such a young age. He will be a great catch for some young lady one day, she thought. And as had been the case with Jerry, Deidre believed she could help to mold him into the ultimate lover, for the enjoyment of his future lovers.

After about an hour had passed, with Nate and Deidre lounging in the cooling pool water, the duo decided that the cooling water and air temperatures had caused enough body pruning and shrinkage, and they got out to dry off and warm up.

With dry towels wrapped around them now, Deidre led Nate into her bedroom. Everything in her being told her that Nate had really enjoyed the pool escapades and would be wanting more of the same on dry land now. And since Deidre was going to have to get caught up on some work early in the morning, she was eager to get on with the party, so to speak. What in the fuck is it that causes these intelligent and handsome young men to want to be with me? Deidre queried the universe and herself, many times over.

Nate stood silent and naked, curiously watching Deidre, awaiting further instruction from his teacher. His curly brown hair in glorious disarray matched his playful eyes and facial expression, which she thought resembled that of an eager young buck staring into headlights.

Deidre and Nate continued having sex again in different positions, many of which were new to Nate. And there could never be an educational session completed without Deidre giving her very nubile student an invaluable lesson on the ultimate blow job. This was something that Deidre took her time doing and derived great pleasure from.

And though he clearly enjoyed having his cock sucked, Nate got off the bed, guiding Deidre to the edge of the bed, where he held her legs up in the air and began to slowly enter her. The speed and rhythm of Nate's movement quickened, until the two groaned in one final euphoric, perfectly timed climax, followed by a moment of deafening silence as each of their minds digested those amazing moments they had enjoyed just seconds earlier.

Deidre felt totally satiated now and felt Nate to be on the same plane, as she headed into the bathroom to clean up, offering for Nate to do the same. "Are you hungry?" she asked, reminding herself that she had the "hostess with the mostest" duties.

Nate was already putting on his clothes as he answered, "Yes, but I'll pick up something to go. I have an early morning tomorrow."

"Me too!" Deidre replied, feeling relief that an exit plan was already in progress.

"Can I see you again?" Nate asked.

"I might be able to fit to you in again," Deidre quipped.

"Okay. I'll give you a call tomorrow, if that's all right with you?" he asked.

"Sure," Deidre responded. "We'll touch base tomorrow, then."

With that, and with everyone dressed once again, Deidre and Nate began moving their conversation toward the front door.

"I really, really had a great time, Deidre. I hope to see you again soon," Nate said, making direct eye contact with her.

"We'll talk tomorrow, cutie," Deidre said with a tired smile.

She closed the door behind her new student and made her way to the bedroom after turning off all the lights, and she lowered the stereo volume before straightening her disheveled bedding.

Snuggled beneath the sheets and comforter, Deidre lay in solitary state, rerunning her most recent personal memories video, knowing that she in fact would not be seeing Nate again. "Mrs. Robinson" had done her job. To further lead this tender young man on would be cruel. She would explain it the best way she could tomorrow. She needed to let him down easily, putting the onus on herself, which she could do eloquently.

But at least for tonight, Deidre was happily exhausted and now only needed to get some sleep. Her mind wandered off to thoughts of Thomas, Mr. Leary's very intriguing son, before she fell fast asleep. She was so looking forward to meeting him. There's something different about Thomas….He appears to be soulful and genuine, Deidre thought. I could so see myself with someone like him one day, in a real relationship. And then she fell fast asleep.

Chapter 6
A Delayed Date—And an Indecent Proposal

Nate called early the next day, just as she knew he would. With gentle tact, Deidre explained that it was not good for them to continue seeing each other, that he needed to be with someone more his age. Deidre chose her words carefully so as not to hurt his feelings or make him feel as though she did not like him, or that he was in any way inadequate.

Deidre had had enough life experience to recognize the obvious symptoms of a young lover becoming attached, which Nate quickly exhibited. He was so vulnerable, she knew. She also knew that Nate would confuse the sexual relationship as a love relationship, and that it was important for him to learn the difference between the two. The conversation went well, with Nate seeming to understand and yet still leaving the door open for future evaluation. Deidre knew she would miss his hard body but realized she needed to stop the situation before she caused him any unnecessary harm or hurt feelings. Nate's phone number would remain in her "BTX" catalogue, for now.

After speaking with Nate and reflecting disappointedly on her postponed meeting with Thomas, who she really did want to see, Deidre felt a bit somber. Why is the man whom I don't really want to see always available, while the "right man," the one I seem to fall in love with, is always in some sort of complex relationship? she painfully pondered. The story of my life! And I will probably be alone for the rest of my life, Deidre supposed as she busied herself with paperwork and housework in the early afternoon hours. Much needed to be done before heading to Gregory's for their Sunday cocktail hour and therapy session. But Deidre found it difficult to focus on her regular mundane chores as she daydreamed about what Thomas would be like. He is so sexy, in addition to seeming like a nice guy, she thought.

Deidre was definitely in one of her dark moods, and not

entirely in the mood to meet with Gregory, either. She knew that he would lecture her on both her young lover and the possibility of her venturing into a relationship with a man who had relationship issues already. It was not an uncommon topic between the two, and she figured she already knew that she would receive a scolding from him—and probably deserved it. But I can't help who my heart falls in love with, Deidre thought sadly.

It seemed to Deidre that Gregory lived vicariously through her on many occasions, as his social life was rather mundane and boring. He always appeared to look forward to hearing her outlandish tales and would take a last minute cancellation personally, so Deidre pulled herself out of her mental funk and got ready. Throwing on some very casual clothes—certainly nothing she would normally wear out if she were "on the prowl"—she thought jokingly, Maybe I need to just take a break from men for a few days, as she walked to her car. She was ready to make the drive to Gregory's for an afternoon of cheese, crackers, and wine, to accompany her current whine.

While driving to Gregory's, Deidre called her girlfriend Sandra, whom she had not seen or heard from in about a month. Wow, I haven't even told Sandra about the three-night threesome! she thought as she dialed Sandra's phone, figuring she could use the drive time to get her friend caught up on current affairs.

"Hello," Sandra answered.

"Hey, chica, what's up?" Deidre said. "I'm on my way to my Sunday cocktail hour a/k/a therapy session at Gregory's." The statement immediately caused lighthearted laughter between the two.

"Good for you!" Sandra replied. "I have to work tonight at six o'clock," she said unexcitedly.

"Well then, just maybe I will stop by the bar after Gregory's. I wanted to cancel our rendezvous this week, but I can't bear to disappoint Gregory—you know what I mean, Sandra. But now I can use you as an excuse to get out early. And besides, I have to tell you what happened that night with those two guys across the bar from us. And you have to tell me about your very interesting friend who you were speaking with that night, too!" Deidre said with amusement.

"What the hell, Deidre!" Sandra exclaimed. "I went home alone that night, and you went home with both of those guys?" She sounded frustrated.

Deidre laughed and said, "I'll tell you all about it when I stop by for a drink later. There's way too much to tell you over the phone. And I want to see your face, when I tell you what went on with those two and our glorious three-night and four-day fuck-fest. Bye-bye for now." Deidre hung up the phone, leaving Sandra in frustrated suspense. She couldn't help breaking out in laughter for a few moments before singing along with the car stereo the rest of the way to Gregory's, with her windows rolled down. Sandra is going to shit when she hears these steamy details! Deidre thought, imagining Sandra's response when she disclosed the devilishly delicious details.

After happily accompanying several melodies, Deidre finally pulled into Gregory's circular driveway, smiling as she admired his unique and beautiful landscaping. Gregory had skillfully choreographed the planting of colorful trees, flowers, and shrubs, successfully creating a Zen-like ambience of serenity and tranquility. Deidre loved to sit on the unusual stone bench next to the small pond and watch the brightly colored koi as they tranquilly swam about. I am definitely in a better place now than I was earlier, she thought as she paused in the car to take in the surrounding beauty. Views like this transported her mind to only the happiest places.

Letting herself into Gregory's home, Deidre now felt somewhat lighter at heart. She knew that he so relished her visits, and she would never do anything to break or even so much as injure her precious friend's heart. Both Gregory and Deidre were about the same age, yet Gregory was an old soul and not nearly as wild as she was, she knew.

"Well, there you are!" Gregory exclaimed as he grabbed her, pulling her into a passionate hug, and then planting a giant kiss just below her ear. Deidre quickly turned her face, to avoid his kiss landing her on the lips.

I don't want to have that type of thoughts about you, especially now! Deidre thought, feeling a bit unsettled at the moment and wanting to focus only on fantasies of Thomas for now.

"Come, come, come, Gregory!" Deidre said with a smile, skillfully twisting herself free from his attempted seduction and breaking the awkward moment. She then took an obviously disappointed Gregory by the hand and led him outside to the sofa area on the beautiful porch, where they sat down.

The two friends popped the cork on the bottle of "Ball Buster," a red wine blend that Deidre had brought over several weeks before. Deidre enjoyed the primarily Shiraz flavor it had, while Gregory's picky palate preferred the taste of cabernet it had.

"What in the flying fuck is wrong with you, Deidre?!" Gregory exploded at her, clearly annoyed but still lightly amused after hearing about the latest and youngest addition to her "BTX" list.

"And to top it all off, the wine is nearly gone," Gregory said, holding the almost-empty wine bottle in the air to examine the contents left.

"Hold those thoughts, Deidre. I'll grab another bottle. We'll need it to get through this session!" Gregory exclaimed as he stood up, pausing the talk to head for the wine cooler in the kitchen.

"Sit down, Gregory," Deidre calmly instructed. "I don't want any more wine. Let's just talk. I seriously do not need or want to be lectured right now. I am well aware of how fucked-up I can behave sometimes." Her tone conveyed acceptance of her sometimes poor decision-making skills.

Gregory set the now-empty wine bottle back on the table and returned to his seat. "Honey, you know I'm only concerned for your safety as well as your heart," Gregory said declaratively, making direct eye contact to reinforce his words.

Deidre leaned in and grasped Gregory's hands, holding them gently in hers. "Gregory, I so treasure our amazing friendship. Please promise to remain my friend no matter what," Deidre implored him with soulful sincerity.

"You and I, my love, will remain connected in some capacity throughout the remainder of our lives," Gregory assured her.

"Good friends are so hard to come by, my love," Deidre responded.

"Good friends are hard to come by, my dear, but your lovers are certainly another story!" he quipped sarcastically.

Deidre shrank in her seat with a coy smile as she thought, touché! "Don't be so hateful, Gregory," Deidre added, cupping his face with her hands and giving him a much-needed quick kiss on the lips.

"And now, mi amore, I'm going to take off. I have to stop by Sunrise Cigar Bar and touch base with Sandra. It will take the rest of the night for me to get her caught up, Gregory!" Deidre concluded the awkwardly begun conversation in amusement. "So I'll see you tomorrow at the office, love." Deidre collected her cellphone, purse, and shoes in preparation for her exit.

"Listen, Deidre, you know you can talk to me about anything," Gregory said affectionately. He appeared a bit disheveled not only physically but emotionally as a result of her kissing him.

"I know, Gregory. You are always my pillar of strength," Deidre said with a sweet smile as she walked out the door. Stopping briefly at the edge of the front porch, she turned to see Gregory fondly watching her. Deidre blew him a quick kiss over her shoulder before walking flirtatiously to her sexy muscle car. She truly felt it to be "sex on wheels" when she drove it.

And now, feeling an amount of self-examination and empowerment/liberation, Deidre pulled into her favorite watering hole, the Sunrise Cigar Lounge, a very welcoming place with a motley group of locals, where Deidre's good friend Sandra tended bar. There were the usual friendly faces that she saw daily, as the regulars became somewhat of a surrogate family to those who were lonely and needed a place where they fit in.

"What you havin' to drink, girlfriend?" Sandra asked with candor as Deidre bellied up to the bar.

"It's good to see you, too, Sandra," Deidre said with a smile, returning Sandra's quippy attitude.

"I'm supposed to be happy to see you?!" Sandra flippantly asked.

"Don't be so bitter, Sandra," Deidre said jokingly. "If you wouldn't have gotten preoccupied with someone else, we could have had a foursome that night!"

"So what in the world happened that night? I can't believe I missed out," Sandra inquired, anxiously awaiting the wild details with bated breath. She intently listened, laughing intermittently, clearly in disbelief and shock at what she was hearing. But as erotically exciting as the event's details were, they would be rivaled by what would take place unexpectedly that night.

"Okay, Deidre, let me ask you something: Would you agree to be in a threesome with another woman?" Sandra asked her with directness.

"Holy shit!" Deidre blurted out loud, as her brain in much deeper dialog silently exclaimed, "And I thought I knew my friend!"

Sandra went on to tell Deidre that she had been seeing a guy she really cared about, and that he needed to experience his fantasy of a threesome.

Okay now, so how do I respond to this bizarre proposition?! Deidre probed her own psyche in confused amusement.

"Deidre, listen: The dude's newly single after being married for twenty-something years! He needs to experience this shit and play a bit," Sandra exclaimed, leaving Deidre speechless, wondering what Sandra would be saying or asking her next.

"I want to arrange a threesome for Sean with myself and

someone else I can trust," Sandra said.

"You want to do what? You really are serious, aren't you?!" Deidre was in a state of shock as she realized what Sandra was leading up to.

"Yeah, I want Sean to live out his fantasy of being with two women at the same time!" Sandra's expression was dead serious as she stared at Deidre, who felt sure now that Sandra was feeling her out.

Holy fuck! Deidre thought to herself, but no words came out of her mouth. She had been rendered momentarily speechless.

"It has to be with another female I can trust, Deidre!" Sandra insistently reiterated.

After laughing for a few moments, Deidre asked, "And just where will you find this other woman—on the Internet? Is there a special website for arranging this kind of rendezvous?!"

Looking straight at Deidre now, Sandra said, "I was really wanting you to be the other woman, Deidre. I know Sean thinks you're beautiful and sexy as fuck. And I also know that it would be safe."

Now in a complete state of disbelief and shock, Deidre broke out in a hearty laugh as she exclaimed, "Safe? What the hell, Sandra? You've got to be kidding me?!"   'Oh   come   on, Deidre. It will be fun!" Sandra replied with a light, twisted smile, waiting for Deidre's reaction and response.

Feeling no pain whatsoever at that moment after having consumed a fair amount of wine with Gregory earlier, and one drink since arriving at the bar, Deidre acquiesced. "Okay, I guess that will be the next item I can cross off my bucket list. Why not?! That shouldn't be a big deal after being in a porn video last year!"

"You did what last year?" Sandra probed through hearty laughter.

"Yes, you heard me right!" Deidre snapped back in acknowledgement, as they both continued laughing at the crazy situation and the conversation they were involved in now.

"Sean is coming into the bar tonight sometime before my shift ends. Just hang around, and we can get together once I'm off," Sandra suggested.

Dressed in a cut-off denim skirt and simple camisole, Deidre did not feel properly dressed for such an occasion, and what's more, she knew she had to work the next day. But after consuming several additional drinks before Sandra's shift ended, Deidre had a nice buzz going and couldn't have cared less about what clothes she was or was not wearing.

"Okay, let's go," Sandra said to Deidre as Deidre finished her drink and Sandra's shift ended.

Looking across the bar to see Sean, who was watching her and Sandra as they were talking, Deidre asked, "Is Sean okay with this? I mean, does he know what you are lining up right now?"

"Are you fucking kidding me?!" Sandra replied. She then instructed Deidre, "Leave your car here, and Sean will drive us up to his house. It's about fifteen minutes north of here, and he hasn't had much to drink at all."

I'm so not believing that I've agreed to do this, Deidre thought surreally to herself as the three piled into Sean's Jeep.

With Sean driving, Deidre and Sandra got busy in the back with no hesitation. With Deidre's panties quickly becoming lost, and Sandra's dress now pulled up enough that neither was covered from the waist down, the temperature of all involved was clearly and quickly rising.

Aside from the undirected, cheesy porn video, which Deidre had performed in the year before, she had never been intimate with another woman, and certainly never planned for something like this to happen. But there was something awkwardly enjoyable about this free-love experience, which Deidre found to be liberating, and oh, so taboo. Deidre questioned herself as to whether she would ever even confide the events of the upcoming night with her best friend, Gregory. This is a whole new level of mischievousness, Deidre thought to herself as a Cheshire cat-like grin spread across her face.

As Sean drove down the highway, Deidre could see him glancing up in the rear-view mirror at her and Sandra. Deidre could tell that he was very interested in watching the two of them at play in the back.

Not having experienced an event such as this before, Deidre felt unsure as to whether she should be the one to begin, but she was well aware of what she herself liked and decided to just go with what she felt like doing at that moment. So with Sandra lying on her back on the floor of the Jeep, Deidre slowly began to spread Sandra's legs as Sean drove rather distractedly, viewing in the mirror snippets of the action he was missing.

It felt a little strange to Deidre, but it didn't seem to bother or stop her from trying out this new role. She would put on the performance of a lifetime and maybe even have some fun herself. Sandra lay still as Deidre began exploring her lower half, titillating and focusing on the exact area and tongue action that she herself would enjoy. Sandra's lower body began writhing in response to the attention she was receiving, and she spread her legs even farther in response, and in order to get more.

As Deidre's hands played with her friend's nipples, she buried her face and mouth deeply in Sandra's pussy. The sounds and body movements that Sandra was now making let Deidre know that her friend was enjoying the current performance. A pleasant surprise, Deidre thought to herself, as she appreciated the taste of her friend.

Deidre could feel Sean veer ever so slightly off the road on several occasions as he watched his fantasy unfolding before his eyes, yet behind his current vantage point.

Sean's growing interest was clearly piqued by the loud cries and moans coming from behind him as Deidre successfully thrust her tongue in all the right places, causing this now-challenged chauffeur to need to correct the trajectory of the Jeep a few times.

Her friend's movements and taste alerted Deidre that her friend was nearing orgasm. But without warning, Sandra abruptly sat up and guided Deidre down to the floor of the Jeep, aggressively yanking her skirt off to reveal her freshly shaven barrenness, eagerly awaiting its own action.

Oh my God, this is one of the craziest things I've done yet! Deidre thought, as she felt Sandra getting right down to business. That would be Deidre's business. Deidre experienced a profound realization at that moment: Who better could know a woman's body than another woman, she theorized.

This was certainly not to mean that Dr. Deidre Villanova desired to be with another woman as opposed to a man. Deidre so appreciated the entire erection of a man's body, meaning his building, make-up, and composite. But it did mean that she could better understand and appreciate how same-sex relationships might feel, if only for a few moments. That very erotic educational event in Deidre's personal life would help her as a psychologist, as she felt that now she could better relate to some of her patients of other sexual orientations. She was sure it would prove to be beneficial in a number of circumstances.

Experiencing sensations she had never felt before, Deidre was thoroughly turned on by the whole forbidden situation as she continued indulging in the fantasy's fabrication. She totally enjoyed feeling Sandra lick, suck, and tease all of her tender areas, but Deidre felt that something was missing: a man and his hard dick. This was something that she wanted and needed. But she was sure as hell going to enjoy each and every moment of what, she was experiencing right now.

Deidre was oblivious to the route Sean was driving until the Jeep slowed and began making frequent turns. We must be getting close to Sean's, she surmised, with the Jeep soon coming to a stop.

"We're here!" Sean exulted as he leapt out from the driver's seat and came around to the back of the Jeep, opening the back door. The look of surprise on Sean's face upon seeing both Deidre and Sandra nearly naked and with their hair in disarray was quite arousing.

As she exited the jeep, Deidre perused her rather blurred mental notes for what belongings she might have left inside. She rummaged around the back of the Jeep in the dark, finding it impossible to see or easily locate anything at that time.

Fuck it! she thought to herself, deciding that the milieu at that moment was far more deserving of her focus and attention. I'm sure that Sandra will show up at the bar and in some awkward moment, indiscreetly hand my panties across the bar with a smile, leaving me to answer many a question from innocent bystanders overhearing and observing the interaction. And Sandra knows I'll be left with the task of creatively explaining how she got my panties and why she's returning them from across the bar now. Deidre chuckled to herself, pondering the scenario as she followed Sean and Sandra into the gated yard. She thought it to be a cute little place in the country, with a pool and a friendly older dog, which ran up eagerly to greet them on their arrival.

Sean led a half-clad Deidre and Sandra farther into his privacy-fenced yard, where he set about lighting a fire pit as the two female friends shed the remainder of the clothing they had on. The dewy-damp air brought a chill to the very early morning hours, making the grassy ground surrounding the fire pit a bit too cold to lie directly on.

"I'll be right back," Sandra said before dashing into Sean's home for several blankets, while Sean left to queue up some sounds. Alone and bare now next to the fire pit, Deidre appreciated the moment's tranquil stillness and silence.

Listening to Mother Nature's own surround-sound is amazing, Deidre thought in auditory wonderment as she stood in her own natural nakedness, her body illuminated by the lifelike dancing fire flames. She loved the smell of a fire burning she thought, as she neared it to take advantage of the warmth it offered. The mesmerizing silence was interrupted only by a harmonious melody performed by frogs and crickets off in the distance, blending with the crackling of the fire pit's sweet-smelling embers.

Feeling euphoric and yet a little odd, Deidre reflected on what the plan was and felt a bit strange at how to incorporate Sean, her girlfriend's boyfriend, into the mix and maintain "safety." Deidre figured it might be best to let Sandra make the first move and go from there. She turned to see her friend returning with several large blankets, which the three arranged adjacent the now-blazing warm fire.

Sean returned to the scene within a few moments, completing the trio's head count. The time that Sean had spent driving Sandra and Deidre, witnessing their uninhibited, free-spirited action, had definitely had an effect on him, Deidre realized upon seeing his rigid erection. Oh, this is going to be so interesting! she thought to herself, as Sandra sat down on one of the blankets, glancing up at them as if inviting them to join in.

While Phil Collins's sensual voice sang out, "I can feel it coming in the air tonight, Oh Lord," the opening line of a favorite song of hers, Deidre could smell the sweet fragrance of freshly cut grass. Sandra gently helped her to lie down on the blanket covering the ground next to the fire pit. The seductive sound of the inviting music now joined in voluptuous harmony with Mother Nature, Mother Earth, and a man's fueled fire to set the perfect tone and mood for a deliriously heated session of what Deidre assumed would be fantastic flame-fueled fuckery.

Deidre's total nakedness, mixed with her naiveté regarding such events, left the psychology major to feel as though she herself should not be the one to start interacting with Sean. The situation felt somewhat awkward as Deidre felt no problem in seducing her own man, but the dominant issue at hand was that this was Sandra's man. This was territory that was "off limits," as far as Deidre was concerned. And that uncompromising fact, would create an air of restraint and constraint for Deidre, guiding and guarding her emotions. Her physical motions, were going to be affected. But nevertheless, Deidre would still enjoy herself. After all, how often does an opportunity such as this fall into your lap?!

Deidre noticed a very eager Sean standing nearby, stroking his cock intently, as he watched the two friends openly caressing one another's body with their hands and mouths, leaving no area unexplored, or un-entered. Deidre felt like she was in heaven with the attention her breasts were receiving, until Sandra flipped herself around on top of Deidre in a sixty-nine position.

It was then that she really began to feel a freedom unlike ever before. Thank you, Universe, for allowing me this opportunity and experience! she thought to herself, in seduced euphoria. But the term I would like to really use is that I am just so fucking horny! she self-confessed as she enjoyed that moment of being both a giver and a receiver.

With the further cooling early morning air and the kindling dwindling, the naked trio momentarily halted their escapade mid-scene, to relocate the blankets and themselves to the plush carpeted living room inside. Much better! Deidre thought as she glanced down at her nipples to see they were nearly frozen in the "high beam" setting.

Sandra abruptly excused herself and dashed into Sean's bedroom, returning with a clear plastic storage bin, whose contents shifted about inside as she quickly walked back.

Oh no! Deidre thought to herself. It's going to get even weirder. She laughed aloud with curiosity-driven amusement, heightened with sensual excitement. Both Sean and Deidre focused their attention on what Sandra would retrieve from what was obviously her sex-toy stash. With a devilish grin, Sandra revealed a five-inch vibrator.

Turning the treat on with a twist of its base, and assuming their previous sixty-nine position, Sandra leaned down and licked her friend's now-very moist sweet spot. Deidre felt herself to be in complete, instant ecstasy as she licked and enjoyed Sandra in return. She hoped to stave off her first and most powerful orgasm until she had enjoyed some further action. The temptation to squirt became too great as Sandra fucked her with the vibrator and sucked her clit, but Deidre managed to hold back her grand finale.

While Sandra and Deidre took turns in interesting exploration of one another, Sean lowered himself in to join the two, appearing nervously excited. As Deidre lay supine, with Sandra's pussy entirely and comfortably nestled in her face, Sandra was facing Sean and sucking his cock, using her vibrator as her own cock, to fuck Deidre.

Pulling Sean's cock suddenly from her mouth Sandra screamed, "Yes! Oh fuck, yes!" glancing down at Deidre, who had just pulled the trigger on her friend's impending explosive orgasm. What a wild and free-spirited night! Deidre thought to herself, realizing she was being guided into yet another position.

She found herself bent over the side of the large open end of the sectional couch, to focus on Sandra's pleasure, while Sean prepared himself to enter her from behind. His fingers exploring her wetness, teasing her in a manner she felt was cruelly delicious. This is so wrong, but it feels so fucking good! Deidre thought, struggling with what was right and wrong at that moment. Just stick it in! she screamed inside her own head.

Those eternal-seeming seconds of launch and frustration would become an insignificant memory once Sean spread her backside open and gently guided his nice-sized erection inside her. This must be the truest definition of the term "mind fuck," Deidre's wandering, computer-like brain thought, at a point in time when she was barely able to think rationally at all. Well, if this was a mind fuck, she was reveling in it.

She felt herself in somewhat of a sandwiched position and

94

loved it. She grasped Sandra's thighs, spreading them open and holding on as Sean firmly held on to Deidre's waist for bracing, to ram himself into her now.

"Oh my God, don't stop! Don't stop!" Deidre cried out.

Sandra moaned as her body writhed in response to Deidre's escalating tongue and mouth movements. A connective energy could be felt between the three during those moments of interaction. The trio's adventurous travel would take them to one final erotic destination soon.

Sandra moved into position to lie supine now, so that Sean could enter her missionary style, as Deidre lowered herself onto Sandra's waiting face. This is gonna be a wet one, Deidre knew as she neared an explosive orgasm under the tongue-torture.

The multiplicity of pleasured senses that Deidre was enjoying at that moment during those early morning hours would change her own personal definition of a "mind-fuck" forever, she knew. And as Sean's speed increased and his breathing became louder, Deidre could feel an immense increase in her own pleasure. Sandra's tongue seemed to keep pace with Sean's escalation. Deidre could not believe the nearing sensory overload she felt approaching, with the hedonistic pleasure Sandra's tongue elicited as it jetted in and out of her while simultaneously sucking her enlarged, sensitive clit.

Deidre could sense that Sean was ready to come as he rammed himself at a much faster pace until both he and Sandra came together. They unleashed a litany of sounds as their bodies shook with high-pressured release. The pussy-pummeling mouth-action that Deidre experienced at that time sent her over the edge and into her own magnificently orchestrated climax.

The three exhausted and very hot bodies, now satiated and tired, collapsed haphazardly on the blanket-covered carpeting, each finding a comfortable spot in which to enter their final dimension, a dreamy sleep.

The sun's rise, would arrive much too early for the trio, having just gone to sleep several hours earlier. And the light of day brought a weird sense of reality with it, Deidre thought. Did I really just do what I think I did?! As she pondered that question, she smirked. Well I sure as fuck can't say I wouldn't do that again in the future! She sat up to see Sandra getting up. Sean had quietly slipped out a little earlier, without either of the women knowing. Deidre and Sandra awoke groggily and found their way into the kitchen for coffee, then collected the bedding and strewn toys from the living room floor. The two friends indulged in light humor, and then turned to see Sean coming back inside after loading some items into his car. And in Deidre's sleepy, post-euphoric state, she realized that Sean had her pink thong panties dangling from one finger. He wore a somewhat shy, yet grand smile.

"Give me those!" Deidre said through laughter, with a very reddened face. She snatched them from exhibition as they all continued to laugh. Well, at least I don't have to worry about them turning up at some inopportune moment, Deidre thought to herself as, she secreted herself in the bathroom and slipped them back on beneath her skirt.

Sean needed to drop Deidre off at her car, which she had left at the club the night before. Deidre felt an awkwardness in the conversation between them during the drive back. Both stuck to small talk, with neither so much as even acknowledging any interaction whatsoever, the night before.

"Thanks for everything, Sean. Take care," Deidre said, opening the passenger door and stepping out into the lounge's very empty parking lot in the early morning light. The unwelcome brilliant sun's beams provided an unnecessary spotlight in which Deidre would perform her "walk of shame," hoping to sneak into her home without any nosy neighbors noting her disheveled appearance or recognizing her "night before" clothing. But she needed to hurry. She couldn't be late for her first patient's appointment at nine o'clock, and it was already seven o'clock, she reminded herself.

Deidre was very adept at pulling herself together on short notice. She didn't get overly caught up in bullshit getting dressed and ready for any occasion unless a man was involved. Then she dressed to kill. She also found herself growing increasingly intolerant of those around her who spent so much time disguising themselves and who they really were.

After taking a quick shower, she donned her matching silky chartreuse panties and bra. Deidre wanted to wear a dark, wine-colored, silky button-down blouse with a black pencil skirt that stopped just below her knees. She would accessorize her outfit with a pair of black suede high-heeled pumps and a most unusual necklace, which she did not wear very often.

Deidre only tended to wear her one-of-a-kind special pendant, with its powerful connection to her life and safety, when she was directed to do so by some unknown and unexplainable force in the universe. And this was to be one of those mornings, Deidre felt in a mystic-fog state. The degree of undeniable gravitational pull she was realizing this morning seemed unusually strong.

"Let's not have any drama today!" she said out loud, sighing deeply.

The distinctive, custom-made pendant hung from a very nondescript yet sturdy white-gold chain. The artwork that the chain supported was anything but ordinary, and certainly could not be described as nondescript. This spirit-filled pendant was in the shape of a mermaid, whose real detail and power lay in the stones, which were intentionally joined together for their forces. The body of the mermaid was specifically constructed from peach moonstone for its accurate body hues and its ability to bring out the better part of the people around you, providing positive energy, and unusually divine love.

Light chocolate diamonds were strategically arranged to represent a hair color and flow, similar to Deidre's own. This was one of the few times when Deidre would wear any "bling." But the characteristic properties of this gem were essential to the mermaid, Deidre felt. The energy and healing properties were believed to be strong, with additional powers to bring about growth and wealth.

The accurately chosen emerald eyes of the mermaid were gloriously translucent and piercing. Deidre prided herself in knowing that the emerald was the favorite stone of Cleopatra, the Queen of Egypt, and that it was associated with the goddess Venus and was believed to protect the sanctity of love and faithfulness.

The stone's green brilliance represented Deidre's own rare green eyes with one important exception: the stone's inability to change color. Deidre's green eyes would take on a golden center when her mood became sensual or fiery.

But the believed characteristics of the emerald-green eyes of both Deidre and the mermaid were in sync with one another. From experiencing passionate relationships, to her love of nature, to the somewhat creative and unorthodox way she viewed and lived life, her green eyes were well represented.

Rough-red garnet stones had been used to create a rudimentary scallop-shaped nipple covering for the mermaid, which was not intended to look sensual in nature, although the stone is known for the sensual power it confers on many. The deep blood-red, yet clear, appearance of the garnet is indicative of primordial fire, very strong love, and unification.

The creation of the mermaid's lower body, through her glorious tail, was truly a work of art, well-proportioned in the pendant for its tremendous need in her world. A spectacularly combined azurite and malachite body brought an almost wave-like pattern and feel to the mermaid's body and provided the perfect joining between the stones.

The magnificent finishing touch, seeming to provide the glue that held everything together, could be seen at the very top of the pendent. The mermaid's arms were stretched up toward the sky, gently holding a pink pearl in her hands. A pink pearl, more commonly found in jewelry than the other gem stones, represented the simpler elements in life. The single pink pearl in the mermaid's hands represented the quintessential foundation that all else was reliant on in Deidre's physical and spiritual world. The pink-pearl was believed to possess important powers of faith, kindness, compassion, loyalty, and romance, but even more importantly, protection—something Deidre would desperately need from time to time.

Deidre felt the mermaid itself signified liberation, power, and strength. And by combining the elements of Mother Nature and Mother Earth in the shape of the mermaid, she felt her environment, surroundings, and self to be in balance and even empowered. For whatever reason this morning, she needed to wear her strength-filled siren. And as the day would unfold, she would understand why.

Chapter 7
Danger Invades the Delicious Delirium

In a groggy state of dreamy bliss, still reeling from the effects of the late night before, Deidre felt mentally and physically exhausted. Her thoughts wandered, with a most fantastic fantasy of frolicking further with Sandra and Sean, leaving her smiling.

A brief glance at her reflection in the bathroom mirror displayed a dead giveaway that Deidre was seriously in need of some sleep. After rinsing her face with cold water, she then dabbed concealer where she saw the need. Deidre knew that she would be fast asleep very early tonight, and alone. She would just need to make it through this busy Monday, with a full schedule of needful patients. And that would require her to snap out of the dullness of her senses and focus. For as she also knew, her mermaid had beckoned her, alerted there could be trouble somewhere ahead, very soon.

Deidre grabbed a yogurt to eat later at the office, before performing a cautionary mental check list to be sure she wasn't forgetting anything she needed on this somewhat surrealistic and very sunny morn. The cell phone in her purse suddenly begin serenading and seducing her senses, playing her rock and roller Roger's romantic rhythm, instantly energizing her.

"Wow!" she said excitedly as she fumbled around in her purse to locate the sweet source of the song, which immediately took her thoughts to some very steamy nights with a very hot man.

She answered the phone saying, "Hey there, cutie!"

"I got the concert schedule, and I'd love to see you, beautiful, one of the two nights or both nights that I'm free!" Roger said.

"Can I call you right back, Roger?" Deidre asked quickly. "I'm running crazy this morning and am a little later than I like to be in my mornings' start." She gave a lighthearted chuckle. "We'll have plenty of time to talk while I'm driving to the office," she added, noting a familiar teasing twitch between her legs.

"Sure, no problem!" Roger said, prefacing the duo's disconnect.

Deidre knew she'd feel rushed and distracted if she stayed home to finish the conversation. Instead, she would employ the drive to feel alive, burying any negative thoughts or energies deep away into the archives.

Once inside the car, Deidre buckled her seatbelt before unleashing the engine's roar. With the tremendous power simmering beneath her, she wondered, Why can't I harness the wild mustang I want as easily as I can these 580 horses and their power?!"

Pausing just before engaging the engine into drive, she glanced up at her rearview mirror and began to gently caress her beautiful mermaid necklace. She loved the way it looked on her and how it made her feel. She felt as though she could glean power from it at times when she needed it.

"So far, so good…whew," she stated aloud to herself and the Universe, knowing that there would be something troubling that was imminent but had not yet reared its ugly head. And Deidre also knew that no other human could ever understand her very complex mind as well as her never-ending sexual drive. An innate drive that she would hopefully have satisfied by just one suitor soon. Could Thomas truly be the one? She pondered the question for a brief moment of serious thought before returning her focus to the world around her. He's handsome, sexy as hell, and always well dressed. He's compassionate and kind with his father as well. These were two attributes that were mandatory as far as Deidre was concerned.

I really have been neglecting the yard, she thought as she pulled out of her driveway. Wanting to make a good impression on Thomas, should he ever come to her home. Deidre made a mental note to change out the flowers leading along the walkway up to her front door, and to have the driveway cleaned.

Winding her way through the neighborhood, past the newest preppy cars that sprinkled the preppy 'hood, she remembered that she had reminded herself to call Roger back once she got onto the interstate.

"Hi, Roger. I can't wait to see you!" she exclaimed ecstatically when he answered the phone.

The two continued to discuss the details of their upcoming date, and then they caught each other up on their lives and loves. Roger was so easy to talk to, readily giving Deidre his opinion on her different men through a cloud of smoke and laughter, as they would share a marijuana joint. It was a great no-strings-attached relationship for them both.

A call from Corinne began to beep in on her conversation with Roger. That's weird, she thought. But knowing that she would be arriving at the office momentarily and see Corinne in person in just a few minutes, Deidre decided to spend the last remaining moments of her drive to the office speaking with Roger about good times to come.

Theirs had been an interesting and stress-free relationship, whose only residual ties were heartfelt well wishes at pertinent times. And their steamy rendezvous were filled with great smoke and smoking hot sex. Roger seemed to prefer entering Deidre doggy-style. The size of his enormous cock always left Deidre feeling when they were finished as though her internal organs had been relocated somewhere up near her throat!

One of Deidre's fondest memories was of being with Roger at his place, during the presidential debates. It mattered not to either that Deidre was a Republican, or that her artistically built musician was, not surprisingly, a Democrat. There were no barriers or boundaries between them then, or at any other time. The two herbally numbed themselves as they watched the candidates bantering in their cockfights before them on the boob tube. Deidre and Roger enjoyed each other and explored each other in an exciting sexual and intellectual dance. Exactly the type of dance that Deidre relished yet found to be a rarity. There was nothing better than finding that special someone that you could so easily get lost with, and in. But the two always remained oriented to the fact that theirs would never be a relationship of anything other than exactly that—a sexual and intellectual dance.

The band's pre-recorded audio drowned out the majority of ridiculous rantings, riddled both with righteous and, religious rhetoric. Voiceless yet animated comedic posturing, which the two friends found entertaining.

Deidre was seated on the couch, while Roger sat on the carpeted floor with his back against the couch as he strummed out some of her favorite tunes, while leaning his head back to rest on Deidre's very sensitive inner thighs. She could feel his energy and the strong pheromones circulating between the two, heightening in intensity with the most random of movement.

As she had told Sandra later, "I leaned over his upturned face to visualize and feel his beautiful nakedness further. And as I leaned farther in, he sucked on one of my nipples and sent me into orbit! You can only begin to imagine how spicy things became after that!" She laughed while wearing a very sheepish grin, thinking of many more, undisclosed spicy details.

But thoughts like this were the sort of thing that removed Deidre from her safety zone and sidetracked her sentinel-like sixth sense. Deidre had unfortunately not paid attention to the red flag that had just been raised in front of her. Corinne had called from her own cell phone and not the office phone, which is where Corinne should have called from at this time on a work morning.

Deidre pulled in and parked in her designated space as she was completing her conversation with Roger, and she jotted down the details of their upcoming meeting on an envelope she pulled from her purse.

"Okay, Roger, I'll see you then!" Deidre replied before hanging up the phone and turning her car's ignition off.

Gathering all that she needed to take in to her office, she noted that Corinne's blue Volkswagen was not in the parking lot. Was it this morning that Corinne was going to the dentist? Deidre felt as though she had been so wrapped up in her own life that she had lost touch with so many.

"Why can't I find just one man and be able to settle down and stop all this child's play!" She said in frustration, pounding her hand down against steering wheel.

A text came in just as Deidre stepped out of her car, distracting her thoughts. She was caught up in the moment and headed out to reach the privacy of her office to get her day started. Deidre's introspection caused her to overlook and ignore, important details in her surroundings, things she normally would have been and should have been cognizant of.

But feeling a wave of what she later defined as some degree of unwelcomed paranoia, Deidre extracted her belongings from her car, then opted for a brisker-than-usual stride to her private entrance.

And where is Georgie, the security guard, this morning? It's not like him to miss my arrival and not carry my briefcase into my office? I hope nothing's wrong, She pondered the situation with perplexity.

Still reflecting with a pleasure-filled smile on her conversation with Roger and the night before, Deidre had failed to contemplate the possible reason for Georgie not being at the security gate as usual when she drove through. It was a careless oversight on her part, and not very bright, for someone so well educated and tuned in to the universe surrounding her.

As she walked with her purse in one hand and briefcase in the other, her cell phone began to ring once again, and she felt certain that it would be Corinne. Offloading her cargo onto a planter wall just outside her private door, she answered the phone as she rummaged around in her purse for her office keys. This was yet

105

another mindless oversight on Deidre's part this morning. She always had her office keys ready before she got out of her car. Always.

"Hey Corinne, can I call...." was all she was able to get out before Corinne interrupted her.

"Where are you, Dr. Villanova?! You aren't at the office yet, are you?" Corinne asked in a nervous voice.

"I'm getting ready to go inside, if I can get my damn keys out of my purse!" Deidre declared with exasperation and disoriented annoyance. Her first patient was due to arrive within minutes, and the office should have already been opened with the lights on and coffee made.

What a fucked-up way to start a morning! Deidre thought as their cell phone connection deteriorated, leaving Corinne unable to hear all that Deidre was saying. Deidre's frustration grew as she struggled to decipher the stress-filled fragmented words and staccato sentences spoken by Corinne in warp speed.

But all too late, Deidre did hear Corinne plead, "Dr. Villanova, do not go into the office!" Get away from the building and meet me at the coffee shop around the corner, fast! I will explain everything when you get here."

Corinne was unaware that while she was in mid-sentence, Deidre had located her keys and already entered her office. She was getting ready to punch in her alarm code when she paused and placed her free-hand on her hip continuing to feel increasing perplexity with the evolving events, as she continued her conversation with Corinne.

"Can this morning get any weirder?" Deidre said to Corinne, and then she asked "What the hell is going on, Corinne?"

Upon keenly hearing Corinne's voice now trembling, she listened intently through the bad connection.

"There's something very strange happening, Dr. Villanova. I'm afraid we could be in danger. I'll tell you about Georgie when I see you. Get here quickly. I have already called the first patients of the morning to reschedule them."

"I'll see you shortly, Corinne." Deidre began to feel anxious and to perspire as a strange presence invaded her personal space. Feeling uneasy, but not wanting to panic, she concluded her phone call with Corinne and started collecting her belongings once again, in preparation for leaving to meet up with Corinne, when she heard a single, loud thud, which seemed to come from one of the other offices. Unclear as to exactly where the noise had come from, she stood silently still, frozen in her tracks in front of her desk. She was unsure as to whether she should investigate the sound further, but she opted to play it safe in light of the strangeness the day had already taken on. She stood still and silent for the moment, knowing that she could sprint out her private door quickly if need be.

The office consisted of a traditionally cozy psychologist's waiting room and staff workstation, with three 10-foot-by-10-foot practitioners' offices, which were comfortably and safely decorated. Deidre's office was the farthest down the hallway, allowing her to have her own private ingress and egress, without the patients or their families seeing her come and go. The only other exterior entry to the offices was the one the patients used, leading directly to a discreet and private courtyard entrance designed as such, to protect the identities of many of the VIP patients treated by the practice.

As she eyed the exit just feet away, Deidre carefully contemplated her next move to make a quick exit out the door. And sensing that there could be no oversight on her part right now, she secured her car keys firmly in her hand first. As she turned to leave, the patient entrance door chime suddenly sounded, alerting her that someone had either entered or exited, although she could not tell which.

"Hello? Anybody home?" she heard a man's voice boom from the waiting room area.

"Thomas, is that you?" Deidre asked, feeling some guarded

relief in hearing what she assumed to be a familiar voice.

"Yes, Dr. Villanova. It's Thomas. We're a little early for Dad's appointment, but we got finished with breakfast earlier than expected, so here we are," he said, oblivious to anything that had happened up to that point. Normally, Deidre's private office door and several doors between the waiting area and offices would have been closed, preventing such easy verbal communication. But for some reason they were not, on this very odd morning.

Confused yet gratefully relieved that Thomas was there, Deidre placed her briefcase, purse, and keys on her desk, confused as to how he had been able to get in. She was not aware that anyone had unlocked the front door. And Corinne had told her that she'd rescheduled the morning's patients. But all of that would have to be figured out later. For now, she was just glad that he was there.

Deidre quick-stepped down the short hallway and into the dimly lit waiting room, with just the ambient glow of the ceiling-mounted EXIT sign. She approached the duo in a very restrained state of anxiety, and in a low voice she said, "There's something strange going on, Thomas." Deidre kept her voice low, out of concern that there might be someone else in the office as well. Her concern now, though, was not just for herself but for Thomas and his elderly father as well.

"What's wrong Dr. Villanova?" Thomas asked, oblivious to the morning's strange start.

Unable as of yet to explain all the odd occurrences, and not feeling entirely at ease for the moment, Deidre securely locked the main entry door and told Thomas and his father to follow her, as she hastily returned to her office in the back. She had to retrieve her purse and keys, after which they could exit through her private door.

As they neared her private office Deidre noted that the outside entry door into her office was partially open.

"That's weird. I know I did not leave the door open!" she said emphatically, with increasing confusion and anxiety. "Okay, this is a little too much," she blurted out while panning the desktop for her purse and keys.

"Can you please tell you what's going on?" Thomas asked while helping his father into a nearby chair and then approaching her with seeming desire to help, with whatever the dilemma was. "My purse and keys are missing!" Deidre replied with exasperation as she began searching around her office further.

"Are these what you're looking for?" Thomas queried in a nonchalant, almost humorous manner, as if to dispel her obvious fear, as he bent down and retrieved her purse and jingling keys from the floor, just adjacent to her desk.

"Oh my God! How did they get there? I must be losing my mind!" Deidre retorted with confusion.

Feeling a wave of paranoia and impending danger, Deidre opted for getting everyone out safely and then figuring out what she hoped would be a rational explanation for the morning's oddities.

I have to maintain control! she commanded herself silently. I must call Gregory as soon as I get to my car, she reminded herself. He needs to know about this insanity, and I need him to maintain what's left of mine. With her purse and keys clutched firmly, Deidre approached Thomas and his father in a delicate maneuver of forced calmness—a precarious position to say the least.

"We will speak further outside," Deidre stated as she helped to lift the elderly Mr. Leary up from his seat. Through commanding eye contact with Thomas, Deidre conveyed an important and unspoken message: that they needed to be silent and unquestioning of further details for the moment, a message she reinforced with a forefinger raised to her lips in an unmistakable "Shh!" fashion.

Sensing that Thomas understood the fragility of the unknown current situation, Deidre escorted the group out the already-open door, then locking the door behind them.

"Deidre!" a man's voice yelled out from nearby.

Deidre turned to see a rapidly approaching, very handsome police officer. Well-defined muscles filled out his freshly pressed black uniform nicely.

"Beau, what are you doing here?" Deidre asked, clearly surprised to see him appear at her office. It had been quite some time since Deidre had seen her playful policeman. But an ominous unease would soon replace the millisecond of sexual arousal Deidre had experienced at the sight of her former lover.

"Wow! I'm impressed! This is a great office location!" Beau then immediately got down to business. "We received a report of a cancelled alarm from your office. And since no one can seem to locate the building's security guard, I wanted to check things out for myself," the handsome officer said, with body language and a facial expression that showed concern.

"You mean they can't find Georgie?" Deidre asked. "Oh I'm sorry, Thomas, Mr. Leary. This is Sergeant Gallagher, with the Lawson County Sheriff's Department," Deidre introduced them politely, her eyes never breaking eye contact with Beau's. It was becoming evident that the morning's oddities might not have been just a coincidence.

"May I speak to you privately Dr. Villanova?" the sergeant requested.

"Absolutely, Sergeant Gallagher. Give me just a moment with my patient," Deidre replied, turning now to address Thomas and his father. Deidre could see that Thomas's demeanor had changed during her exchange with Beau, showing that had become clearly uncomfortable with her interaction with the officer, who was talking on his radio as walked away from the group.

"Mr. Leary, I'll give you a call later today and reschedule you for some time tomorrow, if that's all right," she said in a reassuring manner, glancing up at Thomas to be sure that he had heard her message as well.

110

"Please call me if there is anything I can do, Deidre," Thomas said with sincerity, as he gave her a hug, which Deidre took as a sign of his genuine concern. It was obvious that Thomas did not want to leave.

"I will, Thomas. Thank you," Deidre replied.

Deidre was anxious to get back to speaking with Beau, to find out about her beloved security guard, Georgie. But she could also see that the expression on Thomas's face had changed from rising concern over Deidre's safety to a clearly questioning concern about Deidre's obvious familiarity with this handsome officer. Deidre reassured Thomas that all would be fine and not to worry, that she would call him later in the day, and she kissed him lightly on the cheek in appreciation for his concern for her safety.

Deidre called Corinne and apologized for taking so long, stating that she would be there momentarily and to please wait. Hanging up the phone with Corinne, Deidre glanced up to see Beau staring at her in a pleasing manner.

"What in the world has happened to Georgie?" Deidre asked.

"You look great, honey," Beau said with a smile, "but I need to speak business with you first, and then we can catch up." His smirk quickly changed to a solemn expression. "There's something strange going on here, Deidre, and I believe that it just might involve one of your patients." His directness commanded her attention.

"I just got word that Georgie, the security guard, was found tied up in a work shed behind the main building. He wasn't injured, but he was very shaken up. We don't know who the person or persons are who did this. He is at Lawson General Hospital now, getting checked out.

Deidre informed the sergeant of the morning's strange occurrences in her office, bringing added concern to the already-mysterious situation.

"Georgie said that the only thing missing after the abduction was his master keyring, with all of the office building's keys. He said it appeared to be the only thing that the thug was interested in, aside from taking the security guard's security badge."

"Holy shit, Beau!" Deidre blurted out. "That may very well explain how my office was unlocked this morning!"

The duo continued to compare notes, after which Beau informed Deidre that he would be posting extra detail at both her office and her home. He also stated that officers and investigators would be coming to dust for fingerprints, and to view the building's security camera videos carefully. He also instructed her that no one could enter her office without permission in the meantime, and that the investigators should finish everything today.

As Sergeant Gallagher continued scribbling notes on his scratchpad, he looked up at Deidre and said, "We may need access to your appointment book as well, Deidre."

"You know that won't happen without a court order Sergeant Gallagher," she quickly replied, citing patient confidentiality. Then she added with annoyance, "I can't imagine why anyone would have a problem with me!" Remembering and appreciating her fiery personality once again now, as she picked up her purse and other belongings from the hallway bench, Beau reached out and gently placed his hand on her arm and said, "I'm only a phone call away if you need me. I really mean it, Deidre. Any time, day or night."

Their eyes remained locked on one another for what seemed like an eternity, until Deidre began to sense fear in Sergeant Gallagher's demeanor. Instinctively, Deidre felt her neckline for her source of courage, her mermaid. She gently grasped the pendant between her thumb and forefinger, trying to absorb its strength.

"I suppose I won't be able to get back into my office at all until tomorrow?" Deidre inquired with annoyance, pulling herself away from his gripping stare and gravity and returning to her professional persona.

"I'll call you later this afternoon with an update, Deidre," Beau answered.

"This is awful. I'll need to reschedule all of today's patients. I have to meet Corinne and fill her in. Please call me as soon as you know anything," Deidre said as she turned on her heel, breaking the strong pull of Beau's sexual gravity.

Carefully looking around as she entered her car, Deidre glanced up at her appearance in the rearview mirror, to see Beau looking her way as he and another officer stood talking.

Removing her phone from her purse to call Gregory, she realized that she had begun to perspire both from the sun's heat and from running into Beau as well. After starting her car and turning the air-conditioning on, Deidre called Gregory and told him all that was going on. She knew that he would be en route to the office by now and would not be able to get in.

"I'm keeping in touch with a sergeant with the Lawson County Sheriff's Office, who will be updating me on what they find and when we can get back inside, Gregory," Deidre said. She intentionally left the officer's identity out of the equation. She was not in the mood to get into the sordid details with Gregory of her emotionally painful affair at this time.

As she drove to the coffee shop to meet up with Corinne, Deidre rolled her window down and leaned her head on her left hand, feeling the cool breeze on her face and in her hair.

She could never forget what a turn-on it had been, sexting with Beau. The two would exchange numerous erotic texts and pictures during the hours and minutes leading up to his arrival to her home for lunch and dessert each day. By the time Beau would finally make an appearance, she would be perched naked at the top of the carpeted stairs, wearing only stiletto heels, to further heighten the moment's sensual air. I would be so wet by the time that he arrived, she recalled with a devilish grin, remembering how she would leave the front door unlocked, knowing that he was on the way. She loved the way that he would immediately begin to disrobe at the foot of the stairs, leaving her with powerfully seductive sights that she never grew weary of.

She watched with wanton desire as he unbuckled his gun belt and laid it on the couch before undressing at the base of the stairs, in full view, allowing Deidre to appreciate his damn nice physique and his granite-hard cock. The two would then get busy on the carpeted stairs before finishing in the bedroom, and then retreating to the kitchen for a previously prepared lunch and discussions about their daily lives and families.

The circumstances surrounding Deidre and Beau's meeting were interesting. They had been introduced one afternoon by Martin, a mutual friend, just prior to participating in a threesome. And while conversation was limited, the sex was anything but.

Freshly baked Christmas cookies sat perched atop their cooling racks in the kitchen, creating an amazingly scrumptious aroma, filling the first floor rooms and the nostrils of the trio, as they made their way up to Deidre's bedroom.

All clothing fell to the floor as if on cue, with Beau immediately claiming the position he desired, climbing to the top of the bed and lying on his back, beckoning Deidre to get on top of him. She could see his very erect cock was ready for action, while Martin planned his own strategy. She could hear him and feel him behind her, lubricating himself in order to penetrate her anally, a prospect that really intrigued her. It would be the first time she would have two cocks in her at the same time, and she loved the idea.

While Deidre and Beau were enjoying themselves, Martin found himself preoccupied with the awkwardness of the situation and excused himself, leaving the other two to carry on. He would return moments later to the bedside with a smile, a warm cookie, and a glass of milk. Martin sheepishly offered Beau and Deidre a bite of his cookie, annoying Beau, who was not in any mood for a cookie. He wanted only sex at that moment.

"Get the fuck out of here, Martin!" Beau ordered, sending a

chuckling Martin back downstairs while Beau and Deidre finished. Beau then asked Deidre if he could see her again, and then they exchanged phone numbers.

Beau and Deidre would continue seeing each other frequently at lunchtime during weekdays, when she would prepare yummy lunches for them. Of course dessert would be found in the bedroom, afterward.

But somewhere along the line, Deidre fell in love with Beau, who was stuck in a sexless marriage and not getting divorced any time soon. There was a small child involved, and Deidre wanted no part of being a homewrecker, or being a heartbroken mistress. Protecting her heart and pride from any more insult, Deidre ended the affair before it became any more painful than it already was. But memories of their wild playtimes together would always remain fresh in her mind.

It just wasn't meant to be, Deidre consoled herself as she pulled into one of the parking places at the coffee shop to meet Corinne.

Now, I need to focus on figuring out what in the hell is going on at the office, she thought to herself, enjoying a few brief moments in solitude and deep thought, exhausted by the all of the chaos that had already occurred, so early in the morning. She knew that Corinne would be very upset.

Please, Lorelei, Deidre pleaded as she looked in her rear-view mirror once again, gently caressing her mermaid. Please give me the courage to fight whatever, this evil element is. And keep your watchful eyes over me.

Chapter 8
From Foggy Bliss to Near Miss

"Corinne, I know this has been a very stressful morning," Deidre said to her near-hysterical secretary, who rose to greet her with a tight, relief-filled hug, and with tear-soaked napkins clenched in her hand. Residue of mascara-filled tears remained beneath her eyes and on her shirt, leaving no doubt that she had been clearly shaken for some time before Deidre arrived.

Sit down. Take a deep breath. And try to relax," Dr. Villanova directed her.

She realized that it would be far too easy to get a little freaked out herself. Someone needs to be in control and thinking rationally, she realized. She courageously responded to the need in full, Dr. Deidre Villanova fashion. Feeling somewhat empowered now, realizing her protection from the negative forces of the Universe, her Lorelei, was in its proper place, Dr. Villanova gently sat Corinne back down on the bench-seat next to her in the tiny coffee shop and motioned to a waitress standing nearby.

The cute young woman, who gave every appearance of being free-spirited, quickly approached the table, holding a small pen and pad. Eager to write their orders, she asked with a smile, "Would you like to hear our specials for this morning?" disregarding the flashing light in her pocket from her silently ringing cell phone.

"No, thank you," Deidre answered politely; then she requested a bowl of oatmeal with brown sugar, cinnamon, and some sort of nuts — walnuts or almonds. Oh, and would you please bring a side of milk? As well as another cup of coffee for each of us. Thank you so much!" Glancing at Corinne's still-shell-shocked face, Deidre spoke up, breaking the silence to prevent the waitress from exiting as of yet. "At least have a bagel and cream cheese, Corinne," she said with gentle insistence.

"I'm really not very hungry, Dr. Villanova," Corinne solemnly answered, looking from Deidre, then to the waitress, as if she wished not to be questioned further.

"Our bagels are actually pretty good. And we even have several flavored cream cheese spreads," the waitress cheerily chimed in. "My favorite is the brown sugar, with honey and almond spread."

"Now, that sounds good. Can I get that on a poppy seed bagel?" Corinne asked in surrendered interest. She knew very well that Dr. Villanova would hound her otherwise.

"I'll get one for you right now!" the waitress said with a bright and satisfied smile. Her suggestion had piqued Corinne's interest, causing all three of them to smile briefly. The young waitress scurried off to get started on their order.

"Okay, Corinne. So, let's start at the beginning," Deidre said in a guarded and more serious tone.

The atmosphere had lightened somewhat by now and was lacking the earlier anxiety the two women had been experiencing. Corinne began recounting her morning with complete details, some of which were irrelevant. "I got up this morning at six forty-five, as I always do, and turned on the coffee before turning on some music. Some mornings I watch the news, but I wasn't in the mood this morning."

"Just begin where things started getting weird, Corinne," Deidre guided.

Just then they saw the waitress approaching. They paused their delicate-themed dialogue while she served their food. The waitress was more attentive to detail than Deidre would have wished, placing each plate and glass just so. Deidre wanted only for the waitress to hurry up and finish, so Corinne could resume her recounting of the morning's events.

"I'll be back with a warm-up on your coffee in just a minute. Is there anything else I can get you ladies?" the waitress asked considerately.

Deidre glanced around the table briefly and assured her

that they had everything they needed for the moment. Her tone suggested dismissal, though the words in her mind, more blunt, were Yes. We need privacy.

As the waitress left the table, Deidre turned back toward Corinne, placing her right arm around Corinne's shoulder, noting that she was becoming tearful again, obviously still shaken by the morning's events.

Corinne looked directly into Deidre's eyes and said, "I feel so responsible, Dr. Villanova!" The tears resumed streaming down her cheeks.

Frozen in a moment of awkward silence for both, Deidre waited for Corinne to elaborate further as she reached over and gently touched Corinne's hand in a show of support and caring.

"There was a man, Dr. Villanova. He stopped just several car lengths away from where Georgie usually stands at the security booth in the morning. I didn't think too much of it at the time. He rolled his driver-side window down and waved for me to pass him. But as I passed, he looked rather agitated, or maybe angry, but anyhow upset about something," Corinne's expression reflected the growing concern she remembered feeling at the time. "An observation I would have to attribute to you, after so many years!" Corinne added, with a look of admiration toward Deidre.

Leaning in closer to Corinne, Deidre asked, "So what makes you feel in any way responsible for what happened to Georgie?"

With pain-filled eyes as she pulled her face away from Deidre's, Corinne described the disturbing situation. "There was just something odd about his demeanor. I couldn't help notice as I was slowly circumventing his van to get past him and up to Georgie."

She then went on to explain how she realized, as she passed by the van, that it was obvious the man inside it didn't want her to see his face. And that once she had gotten in front of him, she instinctively glanced up into her rear view mirror as she came to

119

a stop next to Georgie. She said it appeared the man was noting her license plate number in his memory and on paper.

"Really?!" Deidre exclaimed with continuing concern and curiosity.

Corinne went on to explain how Georgie did not seem to be the least bit concerned by the occurrence when she commented as she approached him. She said he exclaimed, "'Oh, it happens all the time,'" waving his hand over his head in the air in a gesture of disregard. "He said 'People frequently pull in and turn around, realizing they accidentally turned into the wrong place.'

"It sounded reasonable at the moment, but it certainly didn't explain why he appeared to be writing my license plate number down," Corinne added. Corinne went on to say that she somehow rationalized the situation away, knowing that her mind was always working in overdrive. "After all, he could have been writing anything down, and maybe I was reading too much into the whole situation."

As Corinne continued attempting to wipe away the never-ending stream of tears from her eyes with her napkin, she recounted how she looked back at the little hut where Georgie stood and felt that she had probably seen him alive for the last time. "Nothing seemed inappropriate or out of place, Dr. Villanova!" she stated with a soul-searching expression. "It's just that I felt a cold chill when I drove around him. There was just something weird, something that's impossible to explain, except that I just knew something wasn't right!" She leaned forward and clasped her hands on the table in front of her. Deidre recognized it as the posture accompanying a closing-statement.

"All right," Deidre said while leaning forward to match Corinne's posture. "Now please stop calling me 'Dr. Villanova' when we are in private. I am also your friend." The statement elicited a more visibly relaxed response from Corinne.

Corinne said that it was not until she reached the office and set her stuff down at her desk that she noticed her initial instinct might have been right—that, in fact, something was very wrong. Through her office window she saw the same van stopped at the security gate. And she was sure she saw the same man returning to his driver-side door, after closing the passenger door, but she didn't see Georgie. But, figuring he was simply inside the security booth, she turned her attention to unpacking her lunch and getting ready to call her son, to make certain that he was getting ready for school. The next thing she knew, another tenant in the building called her cell phone, inquiring about where Georgie was.

After receiving no answer several times when she called Georgie's phone, a trembling Corinne said she called the sheriff's office, reporting a potential problem. "I just felt something was very wrong when Georgie didn't answer his phone. I let it ring like crazy! I told them everything that I just told you, Deidre!" She finalized her story with, "I feel terrible!"

Very concerned for Georgie, not to mention the idea that the potentially fatal situation could possibly have been aimed toward them at that moment, and suffering guilt over feeling that she could have and should have done more, it was obvious that Corinne was overwhelmed.

"When I got to the office this morning, the front entrance door was unlocked," Deidre said, waiting intently for Corinne's response, but none came. Finally Deidre continued. "Thomas and his father came in, thankfully. I thought that maybe you'd left the door unlocked." She paused again, still hoping for a response.

"None of this adds up, Deidre," Corinne finally said, while placing her elbows on the table, pressing her fingers into her temples with an expression that bespoke both confusion and deep thought. "Do you really think that someone is really out to harm us?"

Feeling an increasing warmth in her mermaid pendant as Corinne spoke, Deidre was confused as to how she should interpret its message and how to respond. But she did know that

121

the undeniable sensation meant impending danger was nearing in some fashion.

"And by the way, Deidre," Corinne added with the bit of a smirk, "that hunk with the Lawson Sheriff's Department showed up right away when I called."

"Who? Sergeant Gallagher?" Deidre inquired, more than a little curious but keeping her voice level. She could not think of anyone other than Beau whom Corinne might be referring to, but she didn't want to act as if there had been any sort of previous interaction between herself and the handsome sergeant.

"Yes, it was him," Corinne answered.

"That's weird!" Deidre said. "He showed up at the office while I was outside talking to Thomas Leary and his dad. He claimed that he was responding to a canceled alarm and acted as if it was his first trip there." As Deidre's words fell from her mouth, her thoughts wandered in a number of different directions. She could not put them all into an organized fashion.

Deidre told Corinne, "Take the rest of the day off." She was sure her friend needed it. "But let's expect business as usual tomorrow, Corinne." Deidre reiterated the fact that they were overscheduled already, not accounting for emergencies. She looked directly at Corinne and spoke with deliberate intent of how important it was, to get back on track—for both the patients and themselves. "I'll let you know if anything changes. Otherwise, plan on being in the office and ready for patients by nine o'clock. Now go home and get some rest."

Deidre's own mind was working in overdrive. She knew beyond the shadow of a doubt that there was some bad mojo in the air. Her worst struggle for the moment was in determining just which direction this noxious cloud would be coming from. And then, of course, who would be doing this? And why?

After Deidre got Corinne safely tucked into her car and watched her drive away, she turned toward her own parked car, making mental note of her surroundings in case anything else weird were to happen.

Firing up the ignition, she secured her seatbelt and loosened the first few buttons of the silky blouse she had on, just as her Bluetooth connected over to her car's sound system, and her phone began to ring. Figuring it to be Corinne with a question or detail, she immediately answered the call without checking the caller ID.

"How you doing, Deidre?" a familiar man's voice asked, interrupting the song playing on the radio as the call came through.

"Who's calling, please?" she asked coyly, feeling somewhat apathetic. She knew whose voice it was but wished to believe otherwise. Why the hell did I even answer this call?! She chided herself for not paying better attention, knowing that she could not afford to let her guard down, especially with him, if in fact that was who it really was on the phone right now.

"It's Beau," she heard the soft-voiced reply.

"I'm fine, Beau. It's all good," Deidre answered, hoping to thwart any further questioning.

"I would be more than happy to come over personally—and stand guard, I mean," Beau said, sincerity tingeing his voice. He gave a lighthearted chuckle.

"There's no need," she responded calmly, offering no further explanation. She did not wish to rekindle old times, cognizant of the fact that that's all it would be, days gone by, with no hope for any future. Deidre wished for nothing else non-permanent in her life, feeling that she was done with those who were not totally invested, or committed. And with the help of her own personal guardian angel and mermaid, Deidre felt strongly that all would be possible.

As her call with Beau ended, Deidre knew that she had to shake all the thoughts of her previous love, as well as his "BTX" entry. Rolling her windows down and enjoying the pleasant breeze, she indulged in the soothing air and appreciated how it seemed to help clear her thoughts.

With only three or four miles left until she would be home, Deidre felt her biggest concern for the moment was her next day's scheduling and checking on Georgie—not necessarily in that order. She was still not totally convinced that anyone had been intending to harm anyone within her practice, or harm Deidre herself. Not yet.

One more three-way stop and I'm home, she thought to herself, as she slowed for a stop sign. Glancing to her left she saw a car approaching from a distance that posed no problem. But when she looked to her right, her eyes met those of a man who appeared to be staring through her from a distance, making her feel somewhat uneasy. And being a successful psychologist and a very strong woman, Deidre stared directly back, studying the man's face and car, taking in every detail she could in those fleeting moments.

Deidre noted something strange in the man's deliberate stare that did not settle well with her in light of the earlier events. She determined to memorize as much as she could until she reached the safety of her home, and then write the details down. Just in case, she thought to herself.

Deidre made a right-hand turn, opting for a longer-than-usual, route. She figured she could possibly catch a glimpse of the worrisome car's license plate in her rear-view mirror as she passed. But as Deidre turned toward the direction of the car she was going to pass, she looked over to see the driver's window being rolled up. Her vision was now obscured by very dark window tinting. She was now prevented from any further glimpses of the driver. And as she slowly drove past the car, the driver abruptly accelerated through the stop sign, leaving her unable to see his quickly disappearing license plate, as well.

Damn!" She said aloud, as she continued around the longer route to her home. She was not able to determine, at that moment, if the actions of the driver were in fact deliberate or coincidental. There was nothing she could do about it now, she thought while carefully meandering through the neighborhood.

Coming to a stop in her driveway, she quickly scribbled the following details: White BMW with Florida plates. White male. Brownish black hair. Aviator-style sunglasses. There was no way she wanted to risk forgetting any detail, which she knew she might if she waited until later on to document the pertinent details.

Once convinced that every memorable detail was now documented, she turned her car off and collected her belongings. Both mental and physical fatigue were catching up to her quickly. How in the hell can I be this tired so early? she wondered. It was just one more question in a long line of rhetorical questions that she would ask herself, already knowing the answer.

Dragging herself inside her home and feeling somewhat safer upon entry, she still remained threatened by mixed emotions as she dropped her briefcase on the couch and hit the Play-button on her music system. Deidre desired the tranquil sound to invade every corner of her space and mind, to take her away—to transport her somewhere far removed from the stressful events of the day, she thought, while heading to the kitchen to make some herbal tea before calling Gregory and beginning some paperwork.

Lighting seasonally scented candles throughout the house as she always did, Deidre made her favorite herbal tea and grabbed her cell phone to call Gregory. He knew a little of what transpired today and absolutely nothing about the wild threesome she had been involved in the night before. .She was sure she would get an earful after he heard the juicy details. It certainly feels good to think of something pleasant, for a few moments, Deidre thought to herself.

Deidre's candle-lighting was almost ritualistic in nature. She would always start in the kitchen, then the living room, followed by her bedroom. Today she lit a heavily scented candle she had recently purchased. It reminded her of a unique and erotic combination of sandalwood mixed with a fresh seaside fragrance. And as always, the flames danced around the room, keeping time to the hand-picked blues music, perfectly complemented by the special scents.

Glancing over at the Jacuzzi tub, which had been unused for quite some time, Deidre thought, What the hell! as she reached over and turned on the hot water faucet, and then regulated the water's temperature with cold.

As the Jacuzzi tub filled, Deidre took advantage of the privacy and the moment of magical milieu. After kicking off her shoes, she gently removed her mermaid pendant and placed it on her nightstand for the moment. She never left her precious guardian angel unsecured, but she just didn't feel like opening the jewelry safe in her closet right now. She would return her exotic mermaid to its safe stowage and pick up her disrobed clothes after a good soak in the tub.

Standing in front of the bathroom vanity mirror, now loosening her skirt, she allowed it to slide to the floor. Her hips swayed rhythmically as her fingers delicately unbuttoned her silk blouse. With a quick glimpse of the tub showing it was now three-quarters full, Deidre poured in some scented bath salts into the water and then slipped off her blouse and bra, hanging them on the back of the bathroom door. All that was needed now was her phone, herbal tea, and a bath towel. "Check!" she said out loud, noting that all that would be needed would be within her reach as she soaked.

Turning the faucet off, Deidre tested the water temperature with her foot. Finding it to be perfect, she immersed herself with a sigh of relief and immediate relaxation. She was glad that she'd had a Jacuzzi tub put in when she had the home built five years earlier. I should do this more often, she thought to herself, reaping some of its better moments now.

The personal design and decoration of Deidre's bathroom was well blended and meant to be comfortable as well as exquisitely unique. Both New and Old World ideas were combined to come up with an aesthetically pleasing and timeless setting, which joined ocean-flavored accents from around the globe.

And like her precious mermaid pendant, Lorelei, much thought had gone into the materials used as well as their placement, in order to make one feel as though they were in an exotic foreign place, but no one place or time in particular.

Richly colored wall hangings adorned the faux leather-textured deep olive-colored walls, further complemented by the live landscaping brought in by Deidre herself. The tropical plants included bromeliads, small palm trees, and other colorful plants. The Jacuzzi tub was placed in such a fashion that it looked out two French doors and into a privacy-fenced courtyard viewable only from the bathroom. Deidre's attention to detail with respect to forming a continuum between the bathroom and the courtyard was impressive. When bathing, with the doors open, it was almost as if she was outside.

At night, candlelight flickers randomly danced around the room, flashing as they reflected off the various metals in addition to the subtle golden glisten she had added as a very light washed finish on the walls for exactly this purpose.

But as Deidre was taking in the surrounding beauty, thoughts of Beau and how striking he'd looked earlier in the morning played with her mind once again. Why can't I just forget him? I have to get him out of my mind and off my "BTX," listing once and for all, Deidre admonished herself. But how?

The wild times that Beau and Deidre had spent together in years before had been so very good. The intellectual sex between them was nearly as good as the physical, causing an almost irresistible attraction for Deidre. It was such a rarity for her to ever feel such a strong connection to anyone.

Deidre leaned her head back against the tub and relaxed,

allowing the warm, scented bath to envelop her. She just wanted to forget about the events of the day thus far. I really should take some time and go to the gym. A good workout would do me some good right now, Deidre thought to herself, but she did not feel like running into anyone there whom she might know. With her mind in deep thought, she had no desire for any chit-chat right now. And she certainly didn't want to have to explain her day.

After her long soak in the jetted-tub, she decided, she would steal away some precious time, pruning her favorite bushes and trees in the private courtyard off her bathroom.

Why didn't I wait until after I did yardwork to take a long soak in the tub? Deidre chided herself, chuckling at her decision-making skills. But Deidre found caring for her trees, plants, and shrubs to be therapeutic. So she stayed in the water until it finally cooled to an uncomfortable temperature.

Exiting the tub, Deidre dried herself off with a towel before donning a pair of denim shorts and a tank top. With wireless earbuds in, Deidre worked with her plants, keeping up momentum with the music. It was almost like a dance, she felt, trimming the trees and shrubs to certain music. She would get lost in it as though it were a form of art.

Her red Etoile de Holland species of roses had grown heartily on the fence this summer, and the bush was in dire need of trimming and shaping. She was thrilled to see that her pink Comtesse rose bush was full of fragrant flowers. She would be certain to bring in some clippings to brighten up her dining room table.

After several hours, and with the sky slowly beginning to darken, Deidre finished up her work outside, rinsing her feet and hands with the garden hose before gathering her rose clippings and coming in. She loved this time of the year. It was cool enough in the afternoon to get some of her lighter yardwork done without even breaking a sweat.

Walking back through the French doors that led into her bathroom, she headed in to put some of her gardening tools away in the garage. But as she passed through the dining room, she noticed that one of the French doors leading from the dining room to the backyard was ajar. What the hell? she thought as she pulled the door closed, then locked it. A slight chill ran up the back of her neck.

Deidre stood still at the locked dining room door, feeling concerned and a little perplexed as she mentally retraced her earlier steps. Her heart rate increased as she glanced around for her cell phone to call Beau, in spite of the struggle between her heart and her brain with regard to him.

Beau answered Deidre's call on the second ring. And once Deidre reported to him what had happened, he immediately said, "I'll have someone there in just a few minutes, Deidre. Take your cell phone and go out in the front yard until my deputy arrives and does a walk-through to be sure it's safe. Do not go back into the house until the deputy has gotten there. I mean it Deidre! He then instructed her to go outside to the sidewalk in front of her home while on the phone with him.

"Stay with me, Deidre," he said. She could then hear, through his phone, several voices crackling over the radio as Beau requested a detective to go to Deidre's house. Beau disclosed the known details and stated that there might be a suspect inside her home.

That was all Deidre needed to hear to high-tail it out the front door, just as Beau had instructed her, leaving the front door open after her rushed exit. She really hoped that none of her neighbors would notice anything unusual. She did not want to set the scene for a neighborhood drama session for the bored housewives. The litany of concerned phone calls and visits would be so intrusive, in her very guarded personal life and world.

Within just a matter of moments, a well-built, but much too young-looking, detective pulled into Deidre's driveway with his window rolled down.

"Good evening, ma'am, I'm Detective Chavez. Are you Dr. Deidre Villanova?" the obviously adept and adorable officer asked as he began to step out of his patrol car, clearly already confident of being at the correct home. But Deidre knew that Beau had deputies driving past her home already, anyway, so it made sense that he would arrive so quickly, she thought to herself with relief.

After the usual formal preliminary chit-chat between the detective and Deidre, Detective Chavez asked Deidre to stay outside on the sidewalk while he did a walk-through of the home first, before letting her return inside.

"Of course," Deidre said, directing the detective first as to how to gain access to her backyard, where the French door was opened.

Within three to four minutes the detective returned, saying there did not appear to be any signs of forced entry anywhere, and nothing appeared to be broken. He then escorted Deidre inside in order to go room-to-room, for further investigation. Neither Deidre nor the detective could find anything out of place.

A part of Deidre's psyche felt not only violated but moreover assaulted by everything that had occurred during that day, starting with the morning's events and ending with the afternoon's. And feeling instant overwhelming exhaustion now, as some of her fear subsided with the detective there and knowing her home was safe for the moment, Deidre planned on an early bedtime. She just hoped that she would actually be able to sleep through the night.

With her home now deemed safe and secured, the detective and Deidre both came to the conclusion that there was definitely something potentially suspicious about the door being found open; however, the doorknob and bolt lock were both in correct and working order and able to be secured. But they also agreed that Deidre needed to begin taking some extra precautions, in light of the events occurring.

"Thank you so much, Detective Chavez, for getting here so quickly. I must say, I was somewhat uneasy until you showed up," Deidre said with a sigh of relief.

"You can rest easy Dr. Villanova. I am on detail in the area throughout the night, until seven am. And I will make several passes by during my shift," the detective reassured her, handing her his personalized business card with his cell number. "Don't hesitate to call me if anything seems suspicious, Dr. Villanova," Detective Chavez said.

After they said their goodbyes, Deidre secured the deadbolt behind the detective and collapsed onto the couch, gazing at the patrol car's taillights as they disappeared in the distance.

"Fuck the herbal tea!" Deidre blurted out, rising from the couch and heading into the kitchen, now in quest of a glass of wine. A glass of wine and watching the remaining sunset should be enough to put me out tonight! Deidre advised her inner self.

As she watched the quickly evaporating fragments of the sunset caught in the billowy-clouds, Deidre sat in deep thought. She felt somewhat empowered by her handling of the day's events, yet below her "powerhouse" public exterior lay a much more vulnerable creature, a grown woman who shared her innermost secrets with few, if any. Gregory would be the one person most likely to know the most. But she did not tell even him everything. She refrained from telling him things that would hurt his feelings or make him jealous. She was well aware, of his fondness for her and his desire for more than just friendship. The last thing she wished to do was to break his heart or to hurt him in any way.

Now in complete darkness, Deidre carried her empty wine glass back into the house and placed it in the kitchen before heading toward her bedroom, in preparation of an early night's much-needed sleep. But first I have to blow all of the candles out, and I must not forget to put Lorelei away, she reminded herself.

And then I will be ready to drift off into a coma for the entire night! Deidre thought with eager anticipation.

Chapter 9
Could This Be Love...or Just a Loved Lorelie, Lost?

With her eyes heavy, Deidre laid clothes out for the morning, opting for a more conservatively tailored navy blue pantsuit to wear to the office. She paired it with an ivory-colored silky blouse beneath, and comfortable low-heeled pumps. There would be a lot to catch up on at the office due to the events of the day. She had to be on her game.

An avid multi-tasker, Deidre dialed Gregory's number as she made one last trip through her home, making certain that all of her doors were secured and candles extinguished. She needed to update him on the events.

"How you doing tonight, Gregory?" Deidre queried, through a prolonged weary-yawn.

"Well I have certainly been better!" Gregory snapped, in an aggravated tone.

"I know Gregory. It's been one hell of a day, for us all! Just think of poor Georgie!" Deidre said, remembering that she had not yet called the hospital to check on his condition. She also hoped to prevent Gregory from going on with a lengthy dissertation of just how much he had been inconvenienced today. She knew without a shadow of a doubt that the stress she herself, had dealt with topped everyone's involved—except Georgie's, of course.

"But the main reason I called, Gregory, was to tell you that Beau texted me a few moments ago, saying that the investigators were finished at the office. We can get back in the morning at our normal time," she informed him.

"Beau also said that he would personally be there to meet me at the office in the morning to go over the details of the investigation and some safety precautions, in light of the strange things happening" she added. "So I guess we won't know any more until the morning."

"Beau?" Gregory questioned sharply.

"Oh I'm sorry Gregory. I meant to say Sergeant Gallagher, with the sheriff's office," Deidre said nonchalantly, hoping Gregory would not have picked up on her Freudian slip and interrogate her further.

"Well, this whole investigation thing is going to screw my entire week up!" Gregory declared.

Deidre could hear the frustration in Gregory's voice as he continued to vent, saying, "I've managed to fit back into my schedule all but a few of the cancelled patients from yesterday, leaving barely enough time to see the new ones. This is going to be a wild week, Deidre. But I do feel terrible about Georgie! Please let me know what you find out about his condition. And please let him know that we are all thinking of him," Gregory said with sympathy and in finalization of his rantings.

"Oh, and to top it all off, guess what, Gregory? There's going to be a full moon this week, too, so prepare for the event!" Deidre said sarcastically, inciting a bit of laughter from both and ending the call on a lighter note.

Once she had ended her call with Gregory, Deidre located Thomas's phone number, figuring to touch base with him and apologize for the chaos today before falling fast asleep. Let me make my call to Thomas from bed, Deidre thought as she headed to her bedroom.

But before Deidre could finish punching in Thomas's number, she was interrupted by an incoming call from an unfamiliar number. And with everything happening during this crazy day, she figured it was better to take the call. It could be important, related to her office, or to Georgie.

"Hello?" Deidre answered.

"Hey, Deidre. It's Thomas. I had to call you from my father's cell phone. I managed to get water in mine while I was at the beach with my dog earlier this afternoon," he explained.

"Oh no!" She responded, with a chuckle.

As Thomas went on chatting about how beautiful the beach had been earlier in the day, Deidre realized that she had not yet put Lorelie back into her safe place. She glanced over at her nightstand, where she had placed the necklace earlier. She expected to see her colorful guardian angel lying in full view and glistening under the tabletop lamp's light, but she was not.

A wave of panic went through Deidre's entire body and mind instantly. The mere thought of her precious mermaid being gone was beyond her ability to reason with. She instantly went into a mental fog and was unable to focus on anything that Thomas was saying.

"Umm, Thomas? Hang on just a moment," Deidre abruptly said, cutting Thomas off in mid-sentence while she got out of her bed and began walking distractedly around her bedroom, in search of Lorelie.

"Is everything okay?" Thomas asked.

"I'm not sure, Thomas, but I can't seem to locate the necklace that you saw me wearing today," Deidre answered in frustration as she continued looking around her bedroom and then her bathroom. "I know I placed it on my nightstand before I got into the Jacuzzi tub this afternoon." She got down on the floor on her hands and knees to peer beneath her bed and nightstand in the event that it had fallen. But she didn't see how that could even have been possible.

"Oh, now, that sounds nice! A Jacuzzi tub soak would be perfect right now!" Thomas commented in a pleased voice, oblivious to the serious matter at hand.

"It was amazing," she said, unamused and distracted as she frantically looked around her room. All of the relaxation and relief she had felt earlier from having soaked in the Jacuzzi was gone.

"Thomas, I am going to need to call you back. If I cannot find my necklace I will have to call the sheriff's detective again," she said.

"The sheriff's detective?" Thomas asked.

Deidre continued hurriedly looking around her bedroom and bathroom while she stayed on the phone with Thomas. She looked through the clothes that she had taken off earlier, though certain that Lorelie would not be there.

"What type of necklace was it? Was it valuable?" Thomas asked. He was curious but had no clue as to how important Deidre's mermaid was and in so many ways.

In a state of panic, Deidre gave a brief description of her very unique Lorelie and its composition. "The pendant is invaluable!" Tears began to well in her eyes. "It's one of a kind. I had it custom made by a very special man, out of the country. It would be impossible to replicate, Thomas."

Unable to locate her Lorelie anywhere, Deidre sat down on the side of her bed, feeling herself somewhat shaky and overwhelmed. What in the hell did I do with my necklace?! Deidre interrogated herself angrily as tears flowed down her cheeks. She wanted to scream at the top of her lungs but knew it would accomplish nothing except to wake up some of the neighbors.

"Holy shit!" Deidre blurted loudly as she remembered finding the French door ajar earlier. There can be no way that someone actually came inside my home, went into my bedroom, and stole my necklace, Deidre thought in wonderment, How could I have not seen or heard anyone?!

"I should come over and help you search for your necklace, Deidre. And I would like to look around your home myself before you call the sheriff again," Thomas said. She sensed that his concern was not just for the missing necklace but for Deidre herself. She gave him her address. "None of this makes any sense, Deidre," he said before hanging up. "I'll be there in less than an hour!"

Deidre lay still on her bed, re-winding and replaying over and over in her mind the events of the afternoon. Her thoughts were disorganized, and she really didn't feel like entertaining anyone, but she was feeling uneasy and insecure about being alone. She told herself, It would be good for Thomas to come over for a little while.

After putting on a silky sleep shirt and some soft velour pants, Deidre brushed her teeth and hair. She placed a cool, wet washcloth over her eyes to help reduce the swelling produced by prior crying and exhaustion. But while the cool water soothed her swollen eyes, Deidre knew that she needed far more help than just a damp rag to reduce the stress she could see in the mirror. *I definitely will not be winning any beauty pageants tonight!* Deidre jokingly thought as she exited the bathroom, escaping the mirror's unpleasantly reflected reality.

A wave of vulnerability came over her as she entered her living room and busied herself straightening up before Thomas's arrival. *If it weren't for my missing mermaid, I would be more excited to see Thomas,* Deidre thought to herself, turning on some relaxing jazz music as a palliative distraction before haphazardly spritzing on some perfume.

She glanced at the wall clock, figuring Thomas to be arriving within five to ten minutes. It was nearing nine o'clock at night, her workweek bedtime. She thought, *I should check in with the answering service quickly before Thomas gets here.*

"Villanova and Associates. This is the answering service," she heard after several rings.

"Is that you, Olivia? It's Dr. Villanova," Deidre announced.

"Hello, Dr. Villanova. How's your evening going?" Olivia asked. "You don't usually check in this late in the evening. Is everything all right?"

"I hope so, Olivia! It's been a wild day and night! And it ain't over yet! I can certainly tell there's a full moon upon us!" Deidre commented.

"You're not joking, Dr. Villanova!" Olivia chimed in with a chortle. She went on to tell Deidre that someone had called requesting an immediate appointment with her, stating that she told the caller what the office hours were and to call back during regular hours. "I also made it clear, Dr. Villanova, that if it was an emergency they should call 911, but the caller acted annoyed

137

rather than distressed."

Olivia added one final detail that stood out in Deidre's mind, causing her to remember a previously unrecalled detail she had transiently noted but forgotten during her encounter with the strange car hours earlier, on her way home—a car that was driven by an even stranger stranger.

"I couldn't tell for certain whether the caller was a male or female, Dr. Villanova," Olivia reported.

For one millisecond, during Deidre and the stranger's brief StreetSide engagement, Deidre remembered catching a glimpse of what appeared to be a woman's features beneath the masculine hairstyle and a pair of quickly donned aviator-style sunglasses. It had almost appeared as though the stranger had full eyelashes, something more typical of a woman.

Is it possible that the perpetrator is actually a woman? Deidre privately postulated. That particular notion had crossed her mind before.

"Thanks for the update, Olivia!" Deidre responded, with her thoughts focused more now than ever on the events of the day and how they might be connected—the occurrences at the office, the meeting with the strange stranger, and the disappearance of her beloved necklace.

As a last-minute thought, Deidre asked Olivia, "Please do me a favor and text me the number that the caller left, or the number that was on your caller ID."

"They didn't leave a message, Dr. Villanova, and their number showed up on the ID as 'Private,'" Olivia responded.

Deidre was growing increasingly displeased as the moments went by with the sound and mood of this conversation. She knew there had to be a reason that the caller had deliberately made their phone number unavailable.

Before ending the call, Deidre urged Olivia that, should the suspicious caller ever make contact again, Deidre was to be immediately and personally notified even if she was not the doctor on call.

After she hung up, Deidre was unsure as to whether the strange call, strange driver, and even stranger day were really in any way connected—or were they all just part of a bizarre coincidence in an even more bizarre day. And with her Lorelie nowhere to be found for now, Deidre knew that she could not afford to take any unnecessary risks at the moment. However, every inexplicable event needed investigation, she felt, until there was some resolution.

Seated upright on the edge of her bed, Deidre relished the prospect of the solace and safety that she felt assured Thomas's company would bring. But, she thought, she had better check her appearance in the mirror just once more before Thomas arrived.

Keeping direct eye contact with her image in the mirror, Deidre turned her face side to side, assessing the stress damage. Damn! I look terrible! she concluded.

A ding alerted her to a text message on her cell phone. The digits were unfamiliar, and she couldn't recall the number from which Thomas had called her earlier, but the message, "I'm in your driveway," was surely from Thomas. Deidre strode from her bedroom to the front door, hoping to view Thomas through her focusing eye in the peephole. Just as she peered through the peephole, she saw a very handsome Thomas exiting a sexy sports car.

Thank God he's here! Deidre thought, happy that for the moment she was no longer by herself. As she observed the approaching hunk, her inner self had just one thought: Wow! Then her thoughts found voice: "Holy crap!" she exclaimed with nervous excitement at the sight of a casually clad cowboy sauntering toward the closed door.

She had not seen Thomas so dressed down before. But then again, Deidre had only come into contact with Thomas on a professional level prior to now.

Unable to decide whether she was most turned on at the moment by the muscles showing beneath his V-neck white T-shirt, his well-filled denim jeans, or the cowboy boots he had on, Deidre continued secretly spying on Thomas in admiration as he ambulated. Deidre innocently opened the front door, acting surprised just as Thomas was close enough to knock.

Deidre found herself unprepared for the instant and very electrical connection that developed between her and Thomas at a lightning-fast speed. There was something unique about Thomas that attracted her to him fiercely.

What a handsome and nice man Thomas is! Deidre thought as she opened the door wider.

"Well, hello, Deidre. You weren't watching me from the window, were you?" Thomas asked with twinkling eyes and a knowing grin. Caught by surprise with her hand in the cookie jar, Deidre stumbled momentarily for words.

With her eyes big and round as saucers, Deidre organized her scattered thoughts and words as she reached out to grasp Thomas's hand and welcome him into her home.

"Wow! Beautiful!" Thomas exclaimed with a smile as his eyes panned the room. He ended his scan at her welcoming smile.

"Thank you, Thomas!" Deidre replied, still holding onto his hand. They both stood silently in the foyer, with an amazing energy between them. A "cataclysmic connection" was how Deidre had once described that sort of thing to a girlfriend.

"Mi Amor…!" Deidre's heart screamed out. Her skin prickled with goosebumps.

"Oh, excuse me for being so rude, Thomas!" Deidre said, as she regained her composure and released his hand from her firm grasp and before closing the door behind him.

But before she was able to turn back from securing the door, a wonderfully aromatic scent teased Deidre's nostrils, sending her senses wild!

Directing her face in advance of her body, in search of further

140

olfactory and other delight, Deidre observed Thomas's stare, which seemed to be assessing her every move. She felt his precursory stare to be almost predatory in nature. She would be correct in her pre diagnosis of Thomas's potentially well-schemed aspirations. It was obvious to Deidre that Thomas desired to sexually devour her!

Her already-erect nipples were being teased by the silky fabric of her top. She felt a strong draw to this special man whom she had only recently met.

Why didn't I think to put on a bra?! Deidre mentally scolded herself half-heartedly, as Thomas's gaze briefly admired her paired perky protrusions before meeting her in the eyes. Oh boy, he has "that look"! she told herself with amusement.

They both continued to stand in silence, sizing one another up, not knowing of the atomic catalyst preparing to send their senses to seismic levels.

As if on cue, Phil Collins crooned about feeling it coming in the air tonight. This was a song that Deidre knew well and found the lyrics to be very sensual.

She immediately came to the conclusion that their communication would definitely need further investigation—and consummation. For the moment, the stressors of the day had all but fallen by the wayside, much to her delight.

"Well I'm really happy that I came over to check things out for myself," Thomas said, appearing somewhat uncertain as to what to do next.

Deciding to break the awkward moment tactfully, Deidre spoke up, remembering Lorelie. "We have to find my necklace, Thomas. I'll grab a couple of glasses of wine. Would you like white or red?"

The tension Deidre felt at the moment was centered around two quests: to first find her precious necklace, and then to further explore Thomas.

After pouring each of them a glass of white wine, Deidre led the way to search her bedroom, via the dining room, where the duo paused at the infamous French door. Deidre demonstrated and explained the earlier open-door situation, with legitimate effect and affect. It just made it more real, Deidre felt.

"Exactly where and when was the last time you remember seeing your necklace, Deidre?" Thomas inquired, resting his forearms on the back of a lower-profile dining room chair, causing his A-Frame shoulders to show off his "guns." She swore that his weapons became increasingly rigid and sexy in response to Deidre's heartfelt plight.

Although Thomas's body was oh, so sexy, his tone was less than playful. So in spite of how yummy he looked, Deidre realized his first priority and main reason for being there was to secure her safety.

We have to find Lorelie fast! Deidre told herself. I so need to get past this and have some serious relaxation and recreation! A smile teased itself into being across Deidre's lips as she imagined his strong arms and shoulders holding her tightly, making her feel safe. And, how powerful he could be in the bedroom, she imagined. He should definitely be given a "Double XX" rating in my BTX directory, Deidre dreamed devilishly. Decadent fantasies flitted about as her sensual psyche enjoyed itself, licking the sugary sweetness of ecstasy.

Deidre assessed Thomas's additional assets as well, noting a very nice butt. Thomas's stance accentuated his defined masses, muscles, and seemingly chiseled lines.

Now uncomfortably moist between her legs, Deidre led Thomas into her bedroom, showing him the nightstand, where she had exhaustively searched for the carelessly placed precious protector. Deidre fought back the tears that rapidly began to well in her eyes as she spoke.

Turning away from Thomas to face the nightstand, she quickly wiped away an errant tear, not wishing to break down in front of Thomas. But the rapidly increasing pulse of varying emotions coursing through her at the moment overwhelmed her psyche and disarmed her own doctoring instincts.

As she stood silent, quiet and vulnerable, Deidre took a deep breath, attempting to compose herself. She felt two very strong and gentle hands rest on her shoulders as she slowly exhaled. Thomas's unsolicited touch was just what she needed. It was so much more than just hands on her shoulders, she knew and felt to her inner core.

Turning to face Thomas, Deidre felt as though she had been touched by an angel. His face seemed to glow in front of her. It was unlike anything she had ever felt before. She wanted this fantastic feeling to continue as long as possible.

Deidre felt herself being pulled inward both physically and psychologically toward the attractive asylum of Thomas's towering torso. She so needed to, and did, meld herself into Thomas's offer of refuge, with no words necessary between them.

Her mind was in a distant fog with all that had occurred and was occurring. And the positively charged electrical energy that seemed to be all around them created an enigmatic and magical moment of precursory bliss.

A well-cued melodic message echoed through Deidre's body and soul as the soul-filled soloist sang, "I've been waiting for this moment my whole life." In introspection, the erotic and vibrant vibes seemed to have been perfectly chosen for the mood and meeting of eyes and minds.

Deidre felt that she and Thomas were both on the same page as he held her tightly against his chest and gently swayed them both in time to the music.

This is amazing, Deidre thought dreamily, absorbing the support his strong arms afforded.

"Thank you so much for coming over tonight, Thomas," Deidre said softly as she pulled her face from its position of nestling against his sweet-smelling and warm chest, with a bravely surfacing heart.

Deidre used the sultry songs to gently pull herself partially away from Thomas's heavenly grip. She loved how it felt, but having just met Thomas, Deidre felt she had to be careful.

"I know, we need to find Lorelie," Thomas said with sincerity, letting her know that he shared the urgency of her plight. The duo worked together, leaving no stone—or pillow—unturned. But as the night and search continued, there was no sign of Deidre's precious guardian angel anywhere. Nonetheless, she still felt strangely safe with Thomas there.

"I'm not calling the Sheriff's Department again tonight. I just don't have the energy!" Deidre said in resignation. She did not want to talk to Beau, she said. Then she glanced up to meet Thomas's sensitive scrutiny. She could tell that he was speculating on both his and her subsequent sexual moves as well as the satisfying services to be rendered.

This is not at all what I would have expected to be experiencing this evening! Deidre thought with guarded pleasure. For, despite the good feelings that raced through her as a result of Thomas's presence, she could not forget that there remained an evil undercurrent working against her. She had to find out who and why before anyone else got hurt, or something even worse happened, she reminded herself without breaking the mood very much.

"Why don't we sit out by the fire pit for a few minutes and relax," Deidre suggested. She really did need and want Thomas to stay the night with her for several reasons, including feeling safe enough to fall into a deep sleep, which she so needed.

But within seconds, Deidre's ever-ready and sexually charged mind would race immediately to the gutter in a full-color fantasy. The cooler night air had already snapped her sensitive and erect nipples to their fullest salute.

Deidre knew that it would only take the slightest brushing of any part of his beautiful body against one of her breasts when

144

this occurred to set off a chain of events that would rob them both of any chance of restful sleep. For, once Deidre got started with her captivating capture, the only sleep that either would get would be stolen away from the few intermittent respite pauses between adventurous ventures.

Leading Thomas to the outside sofa area, Deidre ignited the fire pit to make the evening's chill a bit more tolerable. She wanted to relax and enjoy what was left of the full moon, brightly illuminating the sky above them. She felt it was portentously romantic.

As they both sat on the outside sofa, sipping their glasses of wine and discussing the day, Deidre felt a sudden cold chill run up the back of her spine. It was not like anything Deidre had felt before, and it made her immediately uneasy. A disturbingly familiar heat developed in her chest at the same time, like the one she felt when Lorelie was sending her a warning. But Deidre was not even wearing her pendant, so how was this even possible, she wondered.

"Wow!" Deidre exclaimed out loud, causing Thomas to shift from his relaxing pose to heightened alert once again. "What is it?!" Thomas asked, attentively postured, awaiting Deidre's explanation.

After deciding against attempting to explain the alerts of impending danger and alarm that she had received, Deidre simply told Thomas that she was too cold and needed to go inside.

The truth be known, Deidre was experiencing an increasingly intolerable chill throughout her body, and she felt an abnormally increasing burning in her chest, which penetrated through to her soul. Since she had just met Thomas, she figured it better not to try to explain the bizarre sensation at this time.

"I'm not comfortable leaving you alone tonight, Deidre," Thomas said as she leaned down to douse the fire pit.

Feeling both exhausted and a little apprehensive in light of the occurrences, not to mention the sensations of warning, Deidre succumbed and agreed with Thomas. She knew that she would sleep better as well with him there.

"Let me show you where the guest bedroom is, Thomas," Deidre said, leading the way down a hallway off the living room. Deidre removed a fresh towel and washcloth from under the vanity and placed it on the towel rack for Thomas as she apologized for being an imposition. She made sure to thank Thomas for being so kind. Deidre was not used anyone— except Lorelie—looking out for her.

"I'm going to sit in the living room and finish my wine, if you'd care to join me, Thomas. But I absolutely have to call the hospital first, to check on the condition of Georgie, the security guard," Deidre said as her eyes panned the room to see that Thomas had all that he needed, before heading back out of the room.

Unable to get an answer on Georgie's cell phone, Deidre spoke with his nurse and was told that Georgie was finally sleeping. Deidre asked the nurse to please let him know that Dr. Villanova had checked up on him. Thomas returned from the bedroom just as Deidre was finishing the call with the hospital.

"Georgie appears to be okay and is sleeping like a baby, according to his nurse. I'll get us some more wine!" Deidre announced as she headed off to the kitchen, returning with the entire bottle. I really shouldn't be drinking this much on a work night. It's going to make tomorrow morning more difficult, Deidre chastised herself.

She felt Thomas was quickly going to move to the top of her BTX list. The romantic vibes he was emitting had turned on all of her senses.

The music played on as Thomas and Deidre sat on the couch, talking. Deidre enjoyed the way the flickering flames danced around Thomas's green eyes, turning them to a richly vibrant golden color.

But the fact that Thomas was still married played a discordant melody in Deidre's mind. Her curiosity finally got the better of her, and she had to ask, "How long have you been married, Thomas? And isn't your wife going to be expecting you home tonight?" Thomas stammered for a moment before answering. She realized she had caught Thomas off guard with her questions, but she had to ask anyway.

"My wife passed away five years ago, Deidre," Thomas answered, watching for her response. "I consider myself to be married," he said, further adding that the term "widower" sounded so morbid and elicited questions he did not care to answer.

"I'm so sorry, Thomas! What happened?" she asked.

Deidre could see the anguish on his face as Thomas gave an abbreviated explanation, saying only that his wife had been involved in a bad one-car accident.

Regretting now that she had brought up the unsettling topic and upset Thomas so much, Deidre moved closer to him on the sofa and placed her hand on his in a show of support and sympathy.

As Deidre witnessed Thomas's struggle for composure, she gave him a loving hug and said exactly what the unflappable Dr. Villanova should say: "I'm here for you if you want to talk. And I'm a good listener, too."

Thomas covered his face with his hands but remained silent. Deidre reached to the side table for a tissue to offer him. "Talk to me, Thomas. Please, let me help you!" Deidre pleaded, her warming arm encircling his shoulder.

Interesting! she ruminated, noting that Thomas had shuddered slightly when she made physical contact with him.

"Are you okay, Thomas? I didn't mean to upset you. And I'm very sorry about your wife. She must have been special to you," Deidre said, noticing a slight relaxation of his tension.

"No, Deidre, it's all right. I really do need to talk about this. Today was a challenging day for me as well," he started, adding how displeased he was at having to leave her at the office alone, earlier in the day. He also spoke up about "Officer whatever- his-name was" being somewhat disrespectful to her.

Deidre was unable to hide a pleased smile at hearing Thomas's remarks in defense of her. She was impressed by his gentility as well as his other notable attributes.

"I appreciate your kindness, Thomas. You're very sweet," Deidre said. Thomas sat upright, appearing to be preparing himself to say something important.

Neither Deidre nor Thomas could have possibly known at that point the magnitude of the impact of their meeting one another. And neither would ever know what had happened to Lorelie.
This was to be an unforgettably fateful day. For as the sun set on one day's scheming, the nightmares to begin the next day were already in the planning stages, however unknown to the two. Fueled by the forces of the moon, an evil undercurrent from another world, located in unfathomable depths of the ocean and universe, had begun to surface once again. And the fact that Thomas and Deidre had met was not part of the plan, which had been carefully laid out.

Thomas seemed to be gathering his strength as he spoke up. "From the first moment I met you, Deidre, you reminded me of Selena. The way you walk, wear your hair, and your smell. I was attracted to you on sight!"

Thomas went on to add, "And we didn't show up early this morning for Dad's appointment by accident." He picked up the now-empty wine bottle, obviously in search of liquid courage.
"Hang on a moment, Thomas. I'll grab more." Deidre dashed to the kitchen and quickly returned with some hastily grabbed crackers, cheese, and another bottle of wine. She had been so preoccupied today that she had not eaten very much, but she began to notice herself feeling a bit woozy, what with all the wine they had already consumed on top of so little to eat.

After placing the refreshments on the coffee table, Deidre turned down the volume on the stereo. She wanted to be able to really focus without distraction on every detail Thomas was getting ready to divulge.

Returning to the sofa, Deidre positioned herself comfortably, facing Thomas. She knew this would not be a short discussion. "There were too many strange things that happened today. Too many to have been a mere coincidence!" Thomas insisted.

Deidre could not have agreed more with Thomas and became instantly fascinated with all that Thomas had to say. Especially when he told her, "Tonight is the anniversary of Selena's accident. And it was a full moon that night too!" He intently locked eyes with Deidre.

"You will find what I have to say hard to believe," he said, pausing and then going on to say, "Just as you seem to, Deidre, Selena had a fascination with mermaids and the ocean. In fact, she would tell me of feeling an inexplicable draw to the ocean during the full moon's three days."

"Really?!" Deidre exclaimed in heightened intrigue, inexplicably eager to hear more.

Thomas recounted how Selena had become obsessed with mermaids, reading and studying all that she could to learn more. He told Deidre that Selena believed there were mermaids actually alive and living deep beneath the ocean, even today.

Their conversation turned to a lighter topic as Deidre and Thomas both shared stories of mermaid sightings they had heard of. But within a few moments, Thomas steered their conversation back in a more serious direction. Deidre attentively listened to Thomas recounting the horrific details of his wife's death, which he shared while staring off into the distance.

"It was one of those nights when she was returning from her weird water pilgrimage, on the final night of the full moon. Her car veered off the road without explanation. Months of heartbreaking investigation could find no cause anywhere."

After a brief pause, Thomas went on softly. "Her car hit a tree. Selena died on impact.

"I can't help but feel somewhat responsible, Deidre. If I had gone with her that night as she requested, she might not have had the accident," he said sadly.

"You might have been killed as well, Thomas," Deidre countered. "Thank goodness you weren't in the car!"

"I just know that I should have been there for her. Just like I knew that I had to come over here and check things out for myself, Deidre. And I'm glad I did!" As he finished speaking, he seemed a bit more relaxed.

"I'm glad you came over, too!" Deidre said with a smile.

The two new friends spent several more hours talking, until Deidre could no longer keep her eyes open. Rising from the couch to carry the dishes and leftover snacks into the kitchen, Deidre lost her balance, tripping over Thomas's shoes in front of the sofa, and landed on his lap.

"Oh my! I am so sorry, Thomas!" a very embarrassed Deidre stated as she looked upward at Thomas, who was smiling down at her as he caught her in a cradling fashion.

Ensnared in a blissfully awkward moment and feeling like a klutz, Deidre had to laugh at herself as she lay on Thomas's lap, staring up at him. She said jokingly, "That certainly was not very glamourous!" as the two erupted into much-needed laughter.
Thomas helped Deidre up from his lap. The two continued to find needed humor in the situation after all they had dealt with that day.

"Let me get those," Thomas offered, reaching for the glasses, as Deidre cleared the plates from the coffee table.

Deidre was impressed with Thomas's manners, helpfulness, and kindness toward her. She couldn't help but smile as she put things away in the kitchen and thought of how she had fallen on top of him. It felt good to be in his arms for those few moments, she thought to herself, as she put the cheese back in the refrigerator.

Closing the refrigerator door, Deidre turned to find herself against Thomas's chest once more, with his welcoming smile and his eyes gazing down on her. She had not heard him coming up from behind her.

"This is ridiculous, Thomas!" Deidre blurted out, unable to stop laughing. But she quickly noticed Thomas was smiling but not laughing with her. Instead, he stood gazing at her with compassion.

Deidre composed herself upon seeing Thomas's deeper and more serious demeanor, realizing herself to be enamored of him. She could not remember ever feeling this comfortable with anyone this fast, she thought to herself. No one had ever captivated her nearly on sight the way that Thomas had. Thomas excited all of Deidre's senses.

The fear that Deidre had felt earlier was all but forgotten for now. And her anxiety had been replaced with a wonderful sensation of butterflies in her stomach, as she and Thomas locked eyes once more, exchanging their excited energies. Looking up at his handsome features, Deidre felt like a young schoolgirl.

"I needed to be here tonight too, Deidre," Thomas said softly and solemnly. "I've only had a few meaningless dates in the past five years, since Selena died. There has been no one who really interested me until you." This revelation rendered Deidre speechless, imagining such a beautiful man being alone for so long.

"You have not only caught my eye, you've piqued my interest! And I must say that the longer I am with you, the more I am intrigued, and want to know more about you!" he said.

"Oh, Thomas, you've been through so much! I am so happy that we met. And I couldn't be happier that you're here, I can't thank you enough!" Deidre said with a gentle smile. She felt an overwhelming chemistry between her and Thomas and was sure his feelings were similar.

"Would it be inappropriate if I kissed you, Deidre?" Thomas asked somewhat teasingly.

Deidre was taken by surprise now by how quickly things were escalating between the two of them, and her knees to begin to tremble. There was nothing that she wanted right now so much as for him to kiss her—well, kiss her and more.

Without warning or waiting for permission, Thomas tightened his grip, giving Deidre a long, passionate kiss, leaving her breathless. She was unprepared for the rapidly escalating pheromones that were teasing her and driving her senses wild.

Deidre could see the burning desire in Thomas's eyes as their epic kiss came to an end. She waited for what seemed like an eternity for his next move, hoping there would be more to come and she would not be disappointed with his hands in coercive control.

Gently clutching her face, Thomas said, "Deidre, you are a very special woman." His lips made contact with her neck, sending shivers throughout her body.

Deidre felt as though she would explode with ecstasy as Thomas teased her neck and throat with his tongue. He continued tickling her to awkward laughter by breathing in her ear.

Erotic emotions between the two were reaching their peak. And Deidre knew that they were on an amazingly sensual course of no return as he sneaked a kiss farther down her neckline, lightly brushing his hand against her wanton nipples. The dampness between Deidre's legs increased as Thomas continued to explore and torment her further with his tongue.

"Do you believe in love at first sight?" Thomas asked with a smile.

Deidre's head and emotions were spinning out of control. Her psyche screamed out for more as her nipples stood on high alert, waiting for additional teasing and titillation.

"I cannot believe it's one o'clock in the morning, Thomas," Deidre stated, as if it were to mean something at that juncture.

"Yes, it is, Deidre!" he replied with a sly smile, disregarding the fact that the next day would be a workday. She knew it would be a very long night and morning. And the wonderfully strange way she felt at that moment excited her much more than the prospect of sleeping!

"So what might you have in mind, Mr. Thomas Leary?" Deidre inquired with a raised brow.

"How about I show you, Dr. Villanova?" Thomas replied facetiously, suddenly scooping Deidre up into his arms and waiting for her response.

Deidre stared up at Thomas in that shared magical moment. She knew that Thomas was also very special, and that he was not like anyone else she had ever met. At the moment, though, she lacked the proper words to respond.

"Well...what do you say?" he asked with soft assertion.

The unrestrained expression in her body language and face spoke for her. A verbal response would have only been wasted energy. Her attentions could be better utilized elsewhere...

Like on his glorious body, she fantasized as he held her stare.

Thomas carried Deidre to the bedroom, placing her gently on the bed with an ambitious smile and a captivating twinkle in his eyes that turned them from their normal greenish-brown to a glowing gold.

One button at a time, please! Deidre's inner spirit cried out in pleasure.

As if on cue, he began unbuttoning his shirt one button at a time, at an agonizingly slow pace. Tormenting her even further, Thomas locked his eyes on hers, holding her captive throughout the entire process. Deidre found it to be one of the most sensual experiences of her life.

As Thomas finished with the lustful loosening of his shirt, she caught a glimpse of his divine chest, further exciting her turbulent loins. But instead of shedding the now-open shirt, he left it on as his hands teasingly moved farther southward. Deidre was unable to keep her eyes off him and his etched chest.

Oh hell no! her psyche shrieked, realizing the prolonged agony she would have to endure. It had taken entirely too long for the shirt. Deidre knew she had to help expedite the painful process and repositioned herself so she was sitting on the side of the bed. "Let me help you with that," Deidre said softly as she began to unfasten Thomas's belt and jeans.

Sliding the zipper of his jeans down, under his approving gaze, she was met with the resistance of his bulge, which was causing tightness in the fabric. She could feel his body twitch with pleasure under her touch as she removed his cargo-confining jeans.

Sensual sighs and heavy breathing were the only sounds in the room as the duo indulged in further exploration and examination of one another, on a much more intimate level. Their bodies pleasurably writhed beneath the covers for hours, until they both collapsed in exhausted satiation.

"Deidre, it's five o'clock. I'm going to have to get going soon," she barely heard Thomas saying softly into her ear from over her left shoulder as they lay in a spooned position.

"Mmmm...," Deidre groaned, feeling his pulsating pressure against her buttocks. Now this is the best wake-up call. My very own "alarm cock," she thought, grinning inwardly as her hips began to move subtly in an agreeable response to the probing, disregarding the early hour and little sleep.

Making the best use of little time would not be a problem for the two new-found friends, who were quickly becoming more than friends. Not one precious moment will be wasted, Deidre assured herself, as their bodies writhed in motions complementary to one another.

"May I see you tonight for a quick dinner?" Thomas inquired, as he began getting dressed to leave.

Without waiting for Deidre's reply, Thomas appealed further, expounding that, "This is an important night, which I would like to share with you."

They agreed on a time for Thomas to pick Deidre up at home in the early evening, before they said a heartfelt "Goodbye."

Though her heart realized a void after Thomas's departure, she could not help but smile after the amazing night and morning they had just shared. He had managed to distract her thoughts and ease her fears. She felt safe, at least for the moment in time. For the first time in Deidre's life, her body, mind, and soul united in the conclusion that she should take a chance with Thomas.

Her morning drive to work would be filled with blissful sensory overload; the grass appeared greener and the sun shone brighter. She reveled in the sight of the beautiful flowering trees that lined the neighborhood streets, which she had not taken notice of before.

Pulling down her visor to quickly check her appearance in the mirror before exiting her car, Deidre spied her own devilish grin staring back.

"Oh boy! I can't be smiling like this all day!" Deidre counseled her excitedly outspoken inner self, knowing that people can be curiously critical as well as envious of such an unrelenting smile. Her mind wandered in wonderful thought and imagination as to what some would speculate as the cause.

Peering at her day's bulging schedule on her computer screen, Deidre glanced through many familiar names and knew what to expect and how to prepare, but the new patients always provided Dr. Villanova a new adventure into the mind's eye. Some had mental disorders, some just needed a reassuring ear and some guidance, while many others were in unhealthy relationships.

"Dr. Villanova, Sergeant Gallagher is here to see you. He said you were expecting him?" Corinne announced.

"Yes Corinne. Show the sergeant in," Deidre instructed her receptionist.

After the usual morning's polite greetings between the two, Beau explained to Deidre that there were no unusual findings or fingerprints in the office or anywhere around where Georgie was found. He stated that the perpetrator was reported to have worn gloves and a hat. He also went on to say that after much review of the surveillance videos, that they were not entirely sure if it was, in fact, a man or a woman who had committed the crimes. So this really could all have been done by a woman? Deidre contemplated with concern.

Beau told Deidre that he would keep her informed of any developments and that she should be on high alert until the case was resolved, leaving her unable to put closure on her fears, especially since Lorelie, her protector, was missing.

"I will put out an alert and call some of the local pawn shops and exotic black market collectors to make them aware of the pendant, Deidre. It's too unique to get very far. I hope you had it insured!" he said in conclusion. But the fact of the matter was not the dollar value of the artistically spiritual creation; it was the invaluable properties that the precious pendant possessed, which she could not seem to explain.

Deidre's next patient came in as Beau was exiting, bidding her good day as he turned on his heel, which no longer appealed to her the way it had before. And even though she was devastated by her missing mermaid, thoughts and fantasies of Thomas began to fill the sorrowful void and distract her from her next patient. She was still distracted when her last patient before lunch, Helene Waldrop, came in with her mundane moaning and life. At last her appointment time was up.

Finally some time for lunch! Deidre thought to herself as Helene stood up from the couch. "I'll see you next week as usual, Helene," Deidre said, concluding their session and then scribbling down some pertinent notes to enter into the computer.

Deidre forcibly stabbed her fork into a clump of salad, carefully targeting a piece of chicken. She was hungry but not much concerned about the taste of her food. She just knew she had been running so hard that she needed some nutrition, especially to be ready for Thomas again tonight.

Pt appears to be maintaining well on current therapy and Rx. No need for change at this time. Will continue to monitor pt status, staying with the current one-day-per-week therapy session was the only entry needed for Helene, Deidre felt

Peering at her computer in a distracted fog of what her evening would hold, she checked her computer entry for errors as she sneaked out a private smile once again more.

Hearing her office phone ringing on her desk, Deidre reached over blindly and punched the familiar speaker button without taking her eyes off her computer screen. She figured it to be a patient issue of some sort.

"I'm confirming a seven o'clock pick-up time for one Dr. Deidre Villanova," she heard a charming voice say playfully.

"Uh—emm—" she laughingly choked out through the food she was swallowing as she wiped her mouth in surprise. "You haven't told me what to wear yet, Mr. Leary! You haven't even let me in on the itinerary."

"Wear something cool, casual, and comfortable that comes off easily!" he instructed her. "But remember to bring a light jacket or sweater. We will end up at the ocean at some point." Her right hand fumbled through her top right desk drawer for a sticky note to write the details on.

Her mind was already busily digesting the intended ocean visit, correlating it to the prior night's talk, when her wandering finger made an inadvertent landing on a cold object farther back in the drawer, with an almost magnetic effect.

"What in the world?!" she said out loud, in a state of electrically charged confusion.

Though curiously bewildered by the icy object, which her now-cold fingers transported into full view, she unwillingly gleaned an insightful warmth that was both inexplicable and irrational in her professional line of thinking. But she found herself completely controlled, attempting to decipher the message that this token seemed to be so desperately trying to communicate to her. She felt it to be a friendly warning—an alarm or wake-up call, if you will.

"Oh shit!" she suddenly blurted out, quickly secreting the token into her pants pocket as her secretary, Corrinne, opened her door, asking if she had finished lunch yet. Yes, it was time for her afternoon schedule to begin and to turn to a blur, as her intrigued thoughts and desires held a grip on her mind.

***

A locally owned and well-frequented seaside restaurant provided the perfect venue for Deidre and Thomas's dinner. By 8:30 in the evening, they had each put away a hearty helping of delicious food and split a bottle of fine wine between them.

Deidre remembered being in awe as to how the candle's flame reflected its wild and wicked dance in Thomas's now-golden-again eyes. She stared back into Thomas's consuming gaze, completely mesmerized by the "one-ness" she felt her soul to be experiencing at that moment.

"Hey, honey, let's head over to the beach now," she heard Thomas say softly as he signed the credit card receipt for their dinner.

Wow! she thought as her psyche snapped its head quickly from side to side in response to the feeling that had just briefly consumed her. Her interrogative brain began to analyze just how any of this could really be happening. None of this is humanly possible! Deidre's brain asserted with vehemence as she got into Thomas's car.

But despite all of the reasonable and rational arguments that Deidre's brain was evidencing against this seemingly supernatural reality, there absolutely could be no denying the increasing warmth she felt in her pants pocket at that very moment. It felt even warmer as her fingertips reached into her pocket, instinctively gripping what lay there without knowing why.

"This is the spot," Thomas stated, suddenly grabbing Deidre's full attention with what she felt certain that he meant. She was afraid of what would come next.

Thomas recalled the skeletal details of the deadly drama that had caused Selena's car to detonate, like a stick of dynamite. He went on, with a rather flat affect, to conclude the painful recounting by saying that the only thing he had left of her from that night was a very strange and special "token" that was miraculously left unscathed by the fatal explosion.

"There was no explainable cause" was the final remark Thomas made before parallel-parking the car in a vacant spot directly in front of the beach.

Deidre's hand felt tiny wave-like surges of a not-unpleasant energy pulsating the entire time Thomas spoke, but in a stronger magnetic fashion than earlier. She was left unsure of what to say or do. And so Deidre opted for remaining silent, as she absorbed every detail Thomas was saying like a totally dried-out sponge with an insatiable thirst.

In addition to finding the rather quiet and somber drive to the beach to be cathartic, Deidre also realized that she had been subconsciously repressing her own deep desire for the ocean until tonight. But why tonight? she silently wondered, safely securing her own token deep down in her pants pocket before she exited the vehicle.

With a small thermal wine pack and basket removed from the trunk in careful clasp, Thomas and Deidre walked down to a more secluded area of the beach. Thomas admitted that it gave him a bit of a melancholy feeling, being there to experience a full moon for the first time since that night.

He laid out a large blanket on the soft sand and set the "goody bags" down. And as Deidre continued to study and surveil the surreal milieu that was quickly surrounding and enveloping her, Thomas was preparing to tease her sensitive senses even further with an epicurean delight—by lamplight, no less!

The full moon's brilliance radiated fluidly across the nearly glass-flat ocean before it bounced around and bedazzled the slowly yet continuously shimmering ripples, which represented waves that would never be, on this evening's aquatic quest.

There was barely an audible sound except the occasional escaping miniaturized rogue wave washing ashore, causing the tiny, comfortably loitering shoreline birds to scurry several inches away to higher ground. No matter how many times Deidre returned to this magical area on the beach, she never tired of its natural beauty nor the beauty of nature that she could feel completely surrounding her.

She became increasingly aware over time that, as she watched the full moon, she would frequently sense a pleasantly warmed and gentle breeze caress her cheek and then sweetly whisper a message before dissipating back into the non-existence whence it had come. Thomas would always be by her side, experiencing his own magical and magnificently star-brightened night, each and every month's full moon.

Deidre retired her dusty BTX list soon after meeting Thomas that night, feeling their relationship quickly blossoming in its unique wonder without either knowing that there had been a carefully planned and metaphysically initiated intervention, painstakingly prepared and executed to unite the two soulmates for this seemingly random special union. But it came at a monumental cost to Lorelie, demanding that her eternal spirit be stripped from her loving Deidre and exiled to the depths of the sea. This way Lorelie would not be able to protect Deidre from the evil forces that sought to keep Thomas and Deidre from uniting.

The intriguing message that Deidre heard whispered wonderfully yet unintelligibly in her ear was the same each time. And though she knew not the message's verbatim content, she knew that it was important enough that it had been sent across many worlds to her ear only. And she knew somehow and somewhere that Lorelie had something to do with it. In that she would find, during the full moon, solace and respite from the darkness-driven manipulative motives of the perpetrators, who would not easily relent in their evil efforts.

But as long as Lorelie could get her message of safety and love across the many worlds that divided them, she would continue to deliver her important message as a kiss, floating safely cushioned on a warm breeze. And as Deidre would feel the breezy kiss, the fingers of her right hand would always be firmly clasping the token, which would always be present in her pocket when she visited the sea.

"Be not afraid, Deidre. I promise to watch over you both always, just as I did your love, Thomas, when I prevented him from entering the car with his beloved wife, Selena, that fateful full-moonlit night. I was only able to spare one of the two of them and had to make a choice. Now go on and live, love, and laugh with your soulmate," was the communiqué, which was translated by the whispering wind as it was transported through her ear's auditory canal and into her head and heart, and then her waiting soul, where none of the eloquence of the message would ever, even once, become lost in translation across or between them or, their worlds.

But Lorelie's powerful spirit would not be laid to rest so easily. She knew that there was far more for her to do in order to protect the so-far-sealed soulmates from the conniving of their enemies in the future. For now, however, she had been exiled somewhere deep below the water's surface and far away from land. It would take a very special hand to bring Lorelie back from the secret location she had been sent to, without succumbing to deadly undercurrents. But she knew it would happen, when the moon and the stars lined up perfectly once again, when the newest protégé had been chosen for her to be assigned to.

Look for the sequel to Pillow Talk, available soon where you bought this book, and get the answers to the questions you are left with.

The following sexual survey was made available to anyone wishing to participate who was twenty-one years of age or older. This survey is by no means scientific, but it is fun and informative.

I regret that there were not the number of survey participants initially intended on, but the animal rescue efforts after Hurricane Maria have kept me in Puerto Rico quite a bit over the past few months. And although the number of participants (thirty) was not great, their answers were!

The respondents ranged in age from twenty-one to seventy-four. Please note that some questions were left unanswered by some respondents.

	M/Yes	M/No	F/Yes	F/No
*Have you experienced an orgasm before?	y	y	y	y
*Have you ever had sex in or on, a car?	16	0	11	2

Additional Comments:

"In a Mercedes Sprinter" (F/24)

	M/Yes	M/No	F/Yes	F/No
*Have you ever had sex on the beach?	16	0	8	4
… In the ocean?	13	3	6	6

Additional Comments

"On the beach in Marco Island." (M/61)
"No, no, no!" (F/70)
"Not yet but I plan on doing it once in my life." (F/26)
"It's on the list!" (F/24)

	M/Yes	M/No	F/Yes	F/No
*Have you ever had sex in a public place?	14	2	10	2
If so, where?				

Additional Comments:

"In public?.... No!" (F/70)
"Yes. Airplane, boat, golf course bathroom, side of the turnpike in a vehicle." (F/57)
"Yes. At a funeral." (M/23)
"Yes. At a Burning Man Festival." (F/33)
"Most exciting at an abandoned house." (F/33)
"At a lifeguard stand." (F/36)
"On a public boardwalk at a beach resort." (F/26)
"Yes. Home plate on a baseball field." (F/55)
"Car parking lot behind a building." (M/54)
"Telephone booth." (M/51)

163

"Had sex in Gander Mountain parking lot." (F/24)
"Had sex in park picnic area in Pensacola, Florida,
and Dean's Rock, in Cape Cod." (M/48)
"Yes. At swing clubs." (M/56)
"Train, plane, bus, beach, woods." (M/61)
"Balconies, Ferris wheel, beaches, hotel pool, etc." (M/61)
"Yes. Concert at Fort Lauderdale Sportatorium. Most exciting in a private plane." (M/59)
"Beach, stranger's driveway, dressing room, lifeguard stand. Most exciting on the hood
and in the back of truck at Hard Rock Casino." (M/32)
"Yes. An alleyway in Spain." (F/56)

*Have you ever been with more than one sexual partner in twenty-four hours?

	M/Yes	M/No	F/Yes	F/No
	13	2	6	7

Additional Comments:

"Ooops! Yes. I was was married and
had a two-year love affair." (F/70)
"At the same time." (F/33)
"My record is three women-Bar pick up,
 'FWB,' and girlfriend. Oddly things like that
 happened more as I got older."
 "Many times." (M/61)
"No-I have a week rule, although it has been
 suggested to me." (F/24)
"Movie theatre, beach, mountain top." (M/36)

*Do you get enough sex from your partner?

	M/Yes	M/No	F/Yes	F/No
	9	7	10	4

Additional Comments:

"No divorced. That's one of the reasons." (M/59)
"I want more sex, but not from her." (M/48)
"Yes, depending on the partner." (M/32)
"Never had gotten enough from any." (F/24)
"I have been fortunate enough to meet my
sexual equal." (F/55)

*What is the ideal number of times to have sex daily for you? (average)

	Male	Female
Once	7	4
2 to 3x	7	4
4+	2	1
Not Daily	0	4

*How many times can you orgasm in twenty-four hours?

	Male	Female
Once only	1	1

164

2 to 3	5	7
4 or more	11	4

Comments:

"17 times in 24 hours at one point in my life." (F/65)
"Just give me 30 minutes between sessions." (F/44)
"During sex "0. During foreplay once." (F/70)
"Like women, men have sexual cycles. At peak, I can usually come 5 to 7 times per night." (M/61)
"I usually orgasm 3 times per session." (F/57)
"Record was 10 to 11. Typical is 2 to 3." (M/48)

	M/Yes	M/No	F/Yes	F/No
*Do you and your partner watch pornography together?	9	7	10	4

Additional Comments:

"Always looking for someone to watch porn with!
(I haven't found them yet)." (F/24)
"I find that almost all the women I know sexually enjoy that-usually accompanied by sex." (M/61)

	M/Yes	M/No	F/Yes	F/No
*Have you and your partner been to a strip club	10	6	8	6
*Had a lap dance together?	9	7	5	9

Additional Comments:

"No, but it would be fun!" (in answer to both). (F/24)
"Yes, Rachel's. It was great steak." (F/26)
"On two occasions I paid a stripper to make my girlfriend cum, while I
watched and helped out." (M/61)

	M/Yes	M/No	F/Yes	F/No
*Have you ever paid for or been paid, for sex?	9	7	2	10

Additional Comments:

"Does sucking it up and getting over the fact that all
I was, was a 'Booty' count? The sex was that good!
So I guess I paid with my pride." (F/24)
"No. But that does not cover the gifts!" (M/61)
"We all pay, one way or another." (M/51)
"Yes.. Mexico." (M/32)
"Been paid." (F/57)
"Was paid as a twelve-year-old prostitute, when I lived on the streets as a child." (F/55)

	M/Yes	M/No	F/Yes	F/No
*Is foreplay important to you, and if so, what type of foreplay do you prefer?				
	14	2	10	2

Comments:

"Depends. Are we "having sex," or making love?" (M/48)

"Good sex is mostly a head game, and it takes time to build up the fantasy. Women in particular
need that. I appreciate it also. The ideal for me is to take woman from reluctance to
enthusiasm to desperation. Actual sex occurs at that last stage." (M/61)

"Love it, but not needed every time." (F/57)

"For foreplay I relax. No point golfing with a Titleist in your shotgun.
My favorites include sexual massage, finger play, and licking, Hitachi vibrator, bondage,
and light spanking/flogging." (M/61)

"Good kissing goes a long way." (M/51)

"Yes. When I like her, I like all of it." (M/23)

"It's my favorite part. So it's very important." (M/36)

"Foreplay prolongs the experience. I like a slow, soft touch." (M/52)

***Favorite type of foreplay listed most frequently by respondents was oral in nature.*

*Do you believe that you experience better sex, as you grow older?

	M/Yes	M/No	F/Yes	F/No
	12	4	9	5

Additional Comments:

"The women know more." (M/59)

"I feel like the best sex was in my 50s. Now I still enjoy it, but not as much as I used to." (F/61)

"My partners are older and much less able to engage in good sex." (F/70)

"I think women are generally less inhibited and more open to new experiences when older. I find the
experience I've gained in knowing what women like makes all the difference and more
outweighs any loss of youthful vigor." (M/61)

"I've grown less shy about what I want and need." (F/24)

"I know what I want." (F/31)

"I have learned more about myself and I
have more experienced partners." (F/26)

"I've become less restrained and willing to try different things." (M/36)

*Do you believe sex to be an important part of a
healthy and cohesive relationship?

	M/Yes	M/No	F/Yes	F/No
	16	0	13	1

Additional Comments:

"Yes, it shows a connection." (F/33)

"It encourages a level of intimacy that would be difficult to achieve without it.
My last 10 years of marriage were sex-free, and that didn't go well. It's part of the five-things that
guys need to stay in a relationship." (M/61)

"I'm a very physical person, so sex is very important to me." (M/36)

*Do you feel comfortable discussing your sexual
needs, desires, and fantasies, with your partner?

	M/Yes	M/No	F/Yes	F/No
	15	1	11	1

Additional Comments:

"Sure. It's part of the foreplay." (M/61)

"Yes., if my partner is comfortable with it." (F/70)

*Do you like to use "toys" in the bedroom?

	M/Yes	M/No	F/Yes	F/No
Additional Comments:	15	1	9	3

"I have two vibrators I like and use." (F/70)
"By myself." (F/36)
"Light bondage." (M/52)
"Absolutely, most always! I used to sell them and have home parties! It was a blast.
 A number of people would speak with me in private about the toys, and how much
 they help. I personally found that once I became comfortable with my own body
 and toys with or without a partner, I smile more often!" (F/55)
"As long as they stay away from me." (M/61)

*How important is it to you to make your partner reach orgasm?

"I want her to be satisfied." (M/54)
"It's never over until my partner cums-preferably multiple times. One of my favorite
 experiences was getting my partner to orgasm so hard she squirted all over the
 bed and made so much noise they summoned hotel security. I managed to untie her
 before they showed up." (M/61)
"Absolutely. It's more important than the act." (M/46)

*Do you have body piercings other than your ears?"

Comments:	M/Yes	M/No	F/Yes	F/No
"11 piercings." (F/31)	1	15	4	10

"4 piercings." (F/44)
"Belly-button and 2x on 'Hood'." (F/55)
"Not opposed to it. Navel and pussy (ouch), piercings are sexy. Tongues not so much." (M/61)

*What is your favorite sexual position?

Men:		Women:	
	Doggie-style 6		Doggie-style 5
	Sixty-nine 2		Sixty-nine 1
	Anal 1		Anal 1
	Oral 1		Missionary 2
	Her on top 2		Her on top 2
	Missionary 1		From side 1

Additional Comments:

"Love sex: Mission/eye contact." (M/48)
"Doggie-style w/restraints for her." (M/61)
"Twisted Sister Swahili Cowgirl Deluxe." (M/61)
"Her on right side, with left leg bent over." (M/52)
"Her legs on my shoulders." (M/51)

*What is the greatest number of partners you have been with in one session?

# of Partners	Male	Female
One	8	6
Two	1	4
3 to 4	7	1
5 or more	1	5

*What is your ultimate fantasy?

Men:		*Women:*	
Multiple Partners 6		Multiple Partners 3	
Love/Romance 4		Love/Romance 4	
Please her 1			

 Additional Comments:
"Staying married and continuing to have good sex with my wife." (M/46)
"Do not need to fantasize about other women. There is only one woman for me." (M/48)
"Pleasing her." (M/52)
"To be with the man I love, and no one else. I have done MOST , and found it to be best
  when you are "in love" with the person." (F/55)
"A healthy, loving sex life with a man worthy of me!" (F/70)
"Bodice-ripping romance!" (F/56)
"To make one million dollars managing a fight and coming home from Las Vegas
  coming home from L in my own plane and then fucking in plane full of $$$." (M/20)
"Getting picked up by older women." (M/25)
"Making love to a redhead, blonde, brunette at the same time." (M/32)
"Threesome w/2 girls. It's happened several times and been amazing. Having both give
  me head while on their knees looking up at me is particularly hot." (M/61)
"I enjoy group sex with another couple. I like seeing my wife pleasured by another
  male, and I would like to do it more often." (M/36)

*What was the greatest age difference of a sexual partner you have been with?
*The males listed the following, as the greatest age difference in years: 8, 13, 14, 15, 20, 22,
23, 25, two were 30, two were 32, three were 35, and one was 40 years in age difference.
The females listed the following: three were 2, one each at 4, 8, 9, 13, 15, 18, 19,
and three at twenty years' age difference. There was one at 40-plus years.*

* *Was it enjoyable?*	M/Yes	M/No	F/Yes	F/No
	15	1	9	4

Additional Comments:
*"Thirty-five years younger. Normally I would not date anyone under 40 though. Not much
  to talk about and you have to show them how to do everything." (M/61)*
"This was not something done for pleasure; I was threatened.
  So NO, I did not enjoy it." (F/55)
"I was 22, and she was 50. I was 44, and she was 31. Both were amazing!" (M/48)
"Absolutely. It taught me a lot." (M/51)

"Not that good. 32 year difference and lack of experience." (M/54) "Eighteen years' difference. LOOOOVVVED it!" (F/24)

*Explain the difference between having sex and making love.
 "...one is exercise." (M/61)
 "Making love has passion and emotion, and hopefully commitment.
  Having sex is to curb an appetite." (F/61)
 "I'd explain, but I'm too hungover." (F/26)
 "By the way you feel afterward." (M/61)
 "There is selfishness in "sex." "Making love" is mutual and passionate." (M/48)
 "There can be mechanical sex, sex with chemistry, or connection. Making love
  has the deepest emotional/spiritual connection." (M/52)
 "Women seem to equate sex and love more than guys do. When sex and love are combined,
  it's amazing, but it's still pretty good when you're just friends." (M/61)

*How old were you when you had your first sexual experience, and was it pleasurable?			M/Yes	M/No	F/Yes	F/No
			10	5	8	6
		Male	Female			
Age in years	12	1	3			
	13	4				
	14		3			
	15	6				
	16	3	3			
	17	1	2			
	18	1	2			
	21		1			

Additional Comments:

"We were scared we would get caught or I would get pregnant." (F/37)
"It was on a friend's couch - with someone on the floor. We had to be quiet.
 And he had "whiskey dick'." (F/24)
"Just finding out what my 'Little Buddy' could do." (M/59)
"I was somewhat disappointed. It wasn't a big deal. I ended up marrying him,
 in part because I had a sexual relationship with him, and I was a "good girl."
 I divorced him after twenty-two years." (F/70)
"It was very traumatic for me, as I was raped at age twelve by an older man." (F/55)
"It was not good. It was my best friend since I was five years old." (F/36)
"An experienced partner really helped. She taught me a lot." (M/61)
"Yes...But guilt." (M/51)
"Yes. She was aggressive but gentle." (M/32)

	M/Yes	M/No	F/Yes	F/No
*Have you ever been in a threesome?	9	7	7	7
*Was it what you imagined it would be?	6	3	5	2

*How many times?		Men	Women
	1-2 Times	4	2
	3-5 Times	3	1
	6 or More	3	2

Comments:

"For five months straight, two-three times per week." (F/33)

"I was so focused on helping the women have a good time that I don't remember
cumming myself, but it didn't seem important at the time." (M/61)

"It was kind of awkward the first time. The rest were pretty fun." (M/48)

"They were all, awkward but fun. Some were even funny! But all in all,
none were anywhere nearly as wonderful as making love to the one you love!" (F/55)

"Hell no, it wasn't enjoyable!" (F/36)

*Have you ever performed in a porn video?	M/Yes	M/No	F/Yes	F/No
"Five years ago." (M/59)	4	12	2	11

"Forty years ago." (M/61)

"With another woman in a bathroom seduction scene that carries into the bedroom." (F/55)

"No. But did a bondage photo shoot with two women in my bedroom. That was hot." (M/61)

*Have you cheated on your current partner,	M/Yes	M/No	F/Yes	F/No
If so, why?	6	10	1	13

Comments:

"No. I love her and would not want to cause any pain or ruin what we have." (M/36)

"Yes. She was sexy." (M/23)

"He knew about it, so I don't consider it cheating." (F/57)

"I had the chance, and I did." (M/61)

"For excitement, pleasure and thrill." (M/54)

"Yes, because I'm an idiot!" (M/46)

"Yes...Because she pissed me off!" (M/32)

"I have in the past...because of a sexless relationship. Later I think it was to
make up for lost time. Since I do not equate sex with love, I guess that was
my rationale." (M/61)

"No. That was the old me." (M/59)

"Yes. Married and don't have sex with wife anymore." (M/56)

"No. No need to!" (M/51)

"No. I can't imagine being with anyone except him." (F/33)

*Why do you believe that many cheat on their partners?

"The relationship lacks commitment." (M/48)

"Lack of communication." (M/52)

"Not being open to their partners sexual needs." (F/57)

"The person's own inability to remain faithful and committed." (F/33)

"No love - You marry someone and are with them for ten years,
and then they change." (F/36)

"Curiosity. They think they are missing out on something." (F/61)

"Not enough sex with partner, unhappy, or acquired feelings for another." (F/26)

"Poor self-esteem, complacency. There are also a number of people I know
who remain in unhappy relationships for a variety of reasons, continuing to
be unfaithful to their partner. Unfortunately, money and other possessions
are valued more to many than respect for their partner, or their own heart and soul." (F/55)

"Because I was lonely after nineteen years of marriage. My lover and I
helped each other survive our lousy marriages." (F/70)

"It's human nature—biologically, mammals are not designed to be monogamous.
Having multiple partners is better for the success of the species. We all have a
biological imperative to procreate with multiple partners to increase the diversity
of the gene pool. Mostly, we are able to fight that imperative, but not always." (M/61)

"For men, they will cheat if given the opportunity." (M/61)

****Most of the answers from both sexes listed the usual litany of reasons for cheating on a partner,
with general unhappiness, boredom and not enough sex being the main reasons listed.
There were also some explanations, which were interesting.*

<u>And finally....What would you like persons of the opposite sex/gender or varying
ages to know about sex?</u>

"Guys are not mind-readers. Most guys I know would prefer to be told that something
works or doesn't. We would prefer to be directed on how to improve, rather than
have the woman fake her orgasm or enjoyment." (M/36)

"If you enjoy yourself, it will reflect to your partner." (F/57)

"We have feelings too! LOL." (M/46)

"Connect... There needs to be an intimate connection, and trust." (F/33)

"It takes two. Intimacy, touching, and kissing.... So much better than wham, bam,
thank you ma'am!" (F/56)

"Have fun with it, it's purely for pleasure. So tend to your partner's wants and needs." (M/32)

"Put some effort into how your partner feels, and experiment more! Don't settle
for mediocre sex. Be more vocal!" (F/24)

"Great stress relief." (F/61)

"Verbal communication is critical to a healthy sex life. Plus genuine caring." (F/70)

"Sex/intimacy is always a "we," situation and not, a "you," or "me," situation." (M/52)

"It's more mental than physical. It all starts in the head, no pun intended." (F/26)

"It's better if you are obssessed and in love with your partner!" (F/31)

"Most women I go out with are close to my age and are pretty sophisticated about
sex. Areas that are sometimes lacking - particularly in younger women include: (M/61)

  * Understanding that sex and love, are different things.
  * Appreciating that good sex is more about the mind than the body.
  * That sex can be fun in all its varieties.
  * That power and sex, are closely related. Sex games that involve the two
    are super hot.
  * Watch the teeth.
  * A good vibrator is as important as a good man.
  * Men are simple creatures. To keep one, you only need to take care of
    five things. Ask me later.

*Thank you to all of those who participated in this fun and informative survey!
I will most certainly do this again, with even more questions, and better formatting.
I hope that you have not only enjoyed reading the responses but have learned a little
something as well!*

www.ingramcontent.com/pod-product-compliance
Lightning Source LLC
Chambersburg PA
CBHW070035260626
47159CB00005B/2045